JAMES PATTERSON is the internationally bestselling author of the highly praised Middle School books, *Homeroom Diaries*, *Kenny Wright: Superhero*, *Jacky Ha-Ha*, and the I Funny, Treasure Hunters, House of Robots, Confessions, Maximum Ride, Witch & Wizard and Daniel X series. James Patterson has been the most borrowed author in UK libraries for the past nine years in a row and his books have sold more than 325 million copies worldwide, making him one of the biggest-selling authors of all time. He lives in Florida.

A list of more titles by James Patterson is printed at the back of this book

first love

JAMES PATTERSON

AND EMILY RAYMOND

PHOTOGRAPHS BY SASHA ILLINGWORTH

1 3 5 7 9 10 8 6 4 2

Young Arrow
20 Vauxhall Bridge Road
London SW1V 2SA

Young Arrow is part of the Penguin Random House group of companies whose
addresses can be found at global.penguinrandomhouse.com.

Penguin
Random House
UK

First published by Century in 2014
This illustrated edition was first published by Young Arrow in 2016
This illustrated edition first published in paperback by Young Arrow in 2017

www.penguin.co.uk

A CIP catalogue record for this book is available from the British Library.

ISBN 9780099567684

Printed and bound by Clays Ltd, St Ives Plc

Penguin Random House is committed to a sustainable future
for our business, our readers and our planet. This book is made
from Forest Stewardship Council® certified paper.

For Jane—

In the fall of 2010, I turned in the outline for
First Love *to my editor, but the story actually
began many years before. I was in love with a
woman named Jane Blanchard. One morning we
were out for a walk in New York City. Seemingly out
of nowhere, Jane suffered a violent seizure. She was
sick with cancer for nearly two years after that, then
died at a young age. Far too young. Janie, I miss
your smile. I hope it lives on in this book, this
love story that reminds me of our time together
(though I don't remember stealing any cars).*

—J.P.

prologue

one

Okay, I may not be putting myself in the best possible light by admitting this, but let me say right at the start that I was such a straight arrow, such a little do-gooder, that skipping my last two classes that day (AP physics and AP English) made me so insanely, ridiculously jittery that it actually occurred to me this whole crazy plan wasn't going to be worth it.

Looking back on it now, I can't believe I was *this close* to backing out of the most beautiful, funny, painful, and life-changing experience I will ever have.

What an idiot I was.

I was at Ernie's Pharmacy & Soda Fountain, and I had about five hundred butterflies throwing an epic party in my stomach. The toes of my vintage Frye cowboy boots kept knocking against the counter, until Ernie—who's about a million years old and pretty much a total grouch—told me to quit it. Ernie is one Nickelback concert away from complete deafness, though, so I took my boots off and kept knocking away.

I was glad he didn't ask why I was sitting in his ancient shop, drinking a giant coffee (which I needed like I needed a hole in the head), instead of two blocks down the street at Klamath Falls High School, listening to Mr. Fox blather on about the space-time continuum. Because what would I have said?

Well, Ernie—Mr. Holman, I mean—I'm waiting for a boy I could never date, and I'm about to ask him to do something so major that it's going to either save our lives or completely destroy us.

Ernie doesn't care much for teen angst, which is probably why practically no one I know ever comes to his shop—that and the fact that all his candy has dust on it and the Snickers bars are hard enough to use as crowbars.

But I don't mind. And neither does the boy I mentioned. Ernie's is *our* place.

That boy had sent me a note earlier in the day. He'd somehow gotten it inside my locker, even though he doesn't go to my school anymore and we have Navy SEAL–type security guards to protect us against God-knows-what (rioting due to sheer small-town boredom, maybe).

Axi—

So, you got earth-moving news, huh?

I'm shocked you think you can surprise me-

or surprised you think you can shock me.

Or something like that.

You're the word nerd.

Well, anyway, can't wait to hear it.

Ernie's. 1:15.

Yeah, that means <u>cutting class</u>.

No excuses.

—Your favorite "scalawag"

That's Robinson for you. I'd jokingly called him a scalawag once, and he'd never let me forget it. He's almost seventeen years old. My best friend. My partner in crime.

I heard the front door open and could tell he'd arrived by the way Ernie's face perked up like someone had just handed him a present. Robinson has that effect on people: when he walks into the room, it's like the lights get brighter all of sudden.

He came over and clapped a hand on my shoulder. "Axi, you dope," he said (affectionately, of course). "Never drink Ernie's coffee without a doughnut." He leaned in close and whispered, "That stuff will eat a giant hole in your guts." Then he straddled the stool next to me, his legs lanky and slim in faded Levi's. He was wearing a flannel shirt, even though it was late May and seventy-five degrees outside.

"Hey, Ernie," he called, "did you hear the Timbers fired their coach? And can we get a chocolate cruller?"

Ernie came over, shaking his grizzled head. "Soccer!" he groused. "What Oregon needs is a pro baseball team. That's a real sport." He put the doughnut on an old chipped plate and said, "On the house."

Robinson turned to me, grinning and pointing a thumb at Ernie. "I love this guy."

I could tell the feeling was mutual.

"So," Robinson said, giving me his full attention, "what's this crazy idea of yours? Are you finally going to apply for your learner's permit? Have you decided to drink a whole beer? Are you going to quit doing your homework so religiously?"

He's always getting on me for being a good girl. Robinson thinks—and my dad agrees—that he's such a bad boy because he quit high school, which he found "insufficiently compelling" and "populated by cretins" (*cretins* being a word that I taught him, of course). Personally, I think he has a point there.

"I'm probably going to fail everything but English," I said, and I wasn't exaggerating. My GPA was about to take a nosedive, because finals were coming up, and with any luck, I wasn't going to be around to take them. A week ago, knowing that would have kept me up at night. But I'd managed to stop caring, because if this plan worked, life as I knew it was about to change.

"Knowing you, that seems highly unlikely," Robinson said. "And so what if you're a little distracted and you—God forbid—get a B plus on something? You're busy writing the Great American Novel—*ow!*"

I'd swatted him on the arm. "Please. Between school and taking care of dear ol' Dad, I haven't had *any* time to write." My dad hit a rough patch a few years ago, and he's been trying to drink his way out of it. Needless to say, the strategy isn't working that well. "Can we focus on the matter at hand?" I asked.

"Which is…?"

"I'm running away," I said.

Robinson's mouth fell open. By the way, unlike yours truly, he never had braces and his teeth are perfect.

"And FYI, you're coming, too," I added.

Two

"DID YOU HEAR THAT, ERNIE?" ROBINSON called. I'd have told him he sounded gobsmacked, but he'd never let me forget that particular vocabulary word, either.

Of course, Ernie hadn't heard anything, not even Robinson's question. So Robinson pushed away the doughnut and stared at me like he'd never seen me before. It's not often I can surprise him, so I was enjoying this.

"Did you ever read that copy of *On the Road* I gave you?" I demanded.

Now Robinson looked sheepish. "I started it…"

I rolled my eyes. I'm forever giving Robinson books and he's forever giving me music, but since he's distractible and my iPod is dead, that's usually about as far as it gets. "Well, Sal—who's really just Jack Kerouac, the author—and his friends go all over the country, and they meet crazy people and dance in

dive bars and climb mountains and bet on horse races. We're going to *do* that, Robinson. We're leaving this dump behind and taking an epic road trip. Oregon to New York City—with stops along the way, of course."

Robinson was blinking at me. *Who* are *you?* the blinks were asking.

I sat up straighter on my stool. "First we're going to see the redwoods, because those things are totally mystical. Then we'll hit San Francisco and Los Angeles. East to the Great Sand Dunes in Colorado. Then Detroit—*Motor City*, Robinson, which is so right up your alley. Then, because you're such a speed addict, we'll ride the Millennium Force at Cedar Point. It goes, like, a hundred twenty miles an hour! We'll go to Coney Island. We'll see the Temple of Dendur at the Metropolitan Museum of Art. We'll do anything and everything we want!"

I knew I sounded nuts, so I spread out the crumpled map to show him how I'd figured it all out. "Here's our route," I said. "That purple line is us."

"Us," he repeated. Clearly it was taking him a while to wrap his head around my proposition.

"*Us.* You have to come," I said. "I can't do it without you."

This was true, in more ways than I could admit to him, or even to myself.

Robinson suddenly started laughing, and it went on so long and hard I was afraid it was his way of saying *No way in hell, you totally insane person who looks like Axi but is clearly some sort of maniac.*

"If you don't come, who's going to remind me to have a doughnut with my coffee?" I went on, not ready for him to get a skeptical, sarcastic word in edgewise. "You *know* I have a terrible sense of direction. What if I get lost in LA and the Scientologists find me, and suddenly I believe in Xenu and aliens? What if I get drunk in Las Vegas and marry a stranger? Who's going to poke me in the ribs when I start quoting Shakespeare? Who's going to protect me from all that? You can't let a sixteen-year-old girl go across the country by herself. That would be, like, morally irresponsible—"

Robinson held up a hand, still chuckling. "And I may be a scalawag, but I am not *morally irresponsible*."

Finally, the guy says something! "Does that mean you're coming?" I asked. Holding my breath.

Robinson gazed up at the ceiling. He was torturing me and he knew it. He reached for the plate and took a thoughtful bite of cruller. "Well," he said.

"Well, *what?*" I was kicking the counter again. Hard.

He ran his hand through his hair, which is dark and always a little bit shaggy, even if he's just gotten it cut. Then he turned and looked at me with his sly eyes. "Well," he said, very calmly, "hell yes."

part one

1

It was 4:30 a.m. when I woke up and pulled my backpack out from under the bed. I'd spent the last few nights obsessively packing and unpacking and repacking it, making sure I had exactly what I needed and no more: a couple of changes of clothes, Dr. Bronner's castile soap (good for "Shave-Shampoo-Massage-Dental-Soap-Bath," says the label), and a Swiss Army knife that I'd swiped from my dad's desk drawer. A camera. And, of course, my journal, which I carry everywhere.

Oh, and more than fifteen hundred dollars in cash, because I'd been the neighborhood's best babysitter for going on five years now, and I charged accordingly.

Maybe there was a part of me that always knew I was going to split. I mean, why else didn't I blow my money on an iPad and a Vera Wang prom dress, like all the other girls in my

class? I'd had that map of the US on my wall for ages, and I'd stare at it and wonder what Colorado or Utah or Michigan or Tennessee is like.

I can't believe it took me as long as it did to get up the guts to leave. After all, I'd watched my mom do it. Six months after my little sister, Carole Ann, died, Mom wiped her red-rimmed eyes and took off. Went back East where she'd grown up, and as far as I know, never looked back.

Maybe the compulsion to run away is genetic. Mom did it to escape her grief. My dad escapes with alcohol. Now I was doing it…and it felt strangely *right*. At long last. I could almost forgive Mom for splitting.

I slipped on my traveling clothes and sneakers—saying good-bye to my favorite boots—and hoisted my backpack onto my shoulder, cinching the straps tight. I was going to miss this apartment, this town, this *life*, like an ex-con misses his jail cell, which is to say: Not. At. All.

My dad was asleep on the ugly living room couch. It used to have these pretty pink flowers on it, but now they look sort of brownish orange, like even fabric plants could die of neglect in our apartment. I walked right by and slipped out the front door.

My dad gave a small snort in his sleep, but other than that, he never even stirred. In the last few years, he'd gotten pretty used to people leaving. Would it really matter if another member of the Moore family disappeared on him?

Out in the hallway, though, I paused. I thought about him waking up and shuffling into the kitchen to make coffee. He'd see how clean I'd left it, and he'd be really grateful, and maybe he'd decide to come home from work early and actually cook us a family dinner (or a what's-left-of-the-family dinner). And then he'd wait for me at the table, the way I'd waited so many nights for him, until the food got cold.

Eventually, it would dawn on him: I was gone.

A dull ache spread in my chest. I turned and went back inside.

Dad was on his back, his mouth slightly open as he breathed, his shoes still on. I put out a hand and touched him lightly on the shoulder.

He wasn't a horrible father, after all. He paid the rent and the grocery bill, even if it was me who usually did the shopping. When we talked, which wasn't often, he asked me about school and friends. I always said everything was great, because I loved him enough to lie. He was doing the best he could, even if that best wasn't very good.

I'd written about eight hundred drafts of a good-bye note. The Pleading One: *Please try to understand, Dad, this is just something I have to do.* The Flattering One: *It's your love and concern for me, Dad, that give me the strength to make this journey.* The Literary One: *As the great Irish playwright George Bernard Shaw wrote, "Life isn't about finding yourself. Life is about creating yourself." And I want to go create myself, Dad.* The Pissy One: *Don't worry about me, I'm good at taking care of myself. After all, I've been doing it since Mom left.* In the end, though, none of them seemed right, and I'd thrown them all away.

I bent down closer. I could smell beer and sweat and Old Spice aftershave.

"Oh, Daddy," I whispered.

Maybe there was a tiny part of me that hoped he'd wake up and stop me. A small, weak part that just wanted to be a little girl again, with a family that wasn't sick and broken. But *that* sure wasn't going to happen, was it?

So I leaned in and kissed my father on the cheek. And then I left him for real.

2

ROBINSON WAS WAITING FOR ME IN THE
back booth of the all-night diner on Klamath Avenue,
two blocks from the bus station. Next to him was a backpack that looked like he'd bought it off a train-hopping hobo
for a chicken and a nickel, and his face made me think of a
watchdog resting with one eye open. He looked up at me through
the steam rising from his coffee.

"I ordered pie," he said.

As if on cue, the waitress delivered a gooey plate of blue-
berry pie and two forks. "You two are up early," she said. It was
still dark. Not even the birds were awake yet.

"We're vampires, actually," Robinson said. "We're just having a snack before bed." He squinted at her name tag and then
smiled his big, gorgeous smile at her. "Don't tell on us, okay,
Tiffany? I don't need a stake through my heart. I'm only five

hundred years old—*way* too young and charming to die."

She laughed and turned to me. "Your boyfriend's a flirt," she said.

"Oh, he's not my boyfriend," I said quickly.

Robinson's response was almost as quick. "She asked me out, but I turned her down."

I kicked him under the table and he yelped. "He's lying," I told her. "It's the other way around."

"You two are a comedy act," Tiffany said. She wasn't that much older than we were, but she shook her head like we were silly kids. "You should take that show on the road."

Robinson took a big bite of pie. "Believe me, we're gonna," he said.

He shoved the plate toward me, but I shook my head. I couldn't eat. I'd managed to keep a lid on my nerves, but now I felt like jumping out of my skin. When had I ever done anything this crazy, this monumental? I never even broke my curfew.

"Hurry up with that pie," I said. "The bus to Eureka leaves in forty-five minutes."

Robinson stopped chewing and stared at me. "Pardon?"

"The *buuuuus*," I said, drawing it out. "You know, the one we're getting on? So we can get the heck out of here?"

Robinson cracked up, and I considered kicking him again, because it doesn't take a genius to tell the difference between being laughed *with* and laughed *at*. "What's so funny?"

He leaned forward and put his hands on mine. "Axi, Axi, Axi," he said, shaking his head. "This is the trip of a lifetime. We are *not* going to take it on a Greyhound bus."

"What? Who's in charge of this trip, anyway?" I demanded. "And what's so bad about a bus?"

Robinson sighed. "*Everything* is bad about a bus. But I'll give you some specifics so you'll stop looking at me with those big blue eyes. This is *our* trip, Axi, and I don't want to share it with a dude who just got out of prison or an old lady who wants to show me pictures of her grandkids." He pointed a forkful of pie at me. "Plus, the bus is basically a giant petri dish for growing superbacteria, and it takes way too long to get anywhere. Those are your two bonus reasons."

I threw up my hands. "Last I checked, we don't have a private jet, Robinson."

"Who said anything about a plane? We're going to take a car, you dope," he said. He leaned back in the booth and crossed his hands behind his head, totally smooth and nonchalant. "And I do mean *take* one."

3

"WHAT ARE YOU *DOING*?" I HISSED AS ROB-
inson led us down one of the nearby side streets. His legs are
about twice as long as mine, so I had to jog to keep up with
him.

When we came to an intersection, I grabbed his arm and
whirled him around to face me. Eye to eye. Scalawag to Ms.
Straitlaced.

"Are you serious about this?" I said. "Tell me you're not
serious."

He smiled. "You took care of the route. Let me take care of
the ride."

"Robinson—"

He shook off my grip and slung his arm around my shoulder, big brother–style. "Now settle down, GG, and I'll give you
a little lesson in vehicle selection."

"A lesson in *what*? And don't call me that." It stands for Good Girl, and it drives me absolutely nuts when he says it.

Robinson pointed to a car just ahead. "Now that, see, is a Jaguar. It's a beautiful machine. But it's an XJ6, and those things have problems with their fuel filters. You can't have your stolen car leaking gas, Axi, because it could catch on fire, and if you don't die a fiery death, well, you're definitely going to jail for grand theft auto."

We walked on a little farther, and he pointed to a green minivan. "The Dodge Grand Caravan is roomy and dependable, but we're adventurers, not soccer moms."

I decided to pretend this was all make-believe. "Okay, what about that one?" I asked.

He followed my finger and looked thoughtful. "Toyota Matrix. Yeah, definitely a good option. But I'm looking for something with a bit more flair."

By now the sun was peeking over the horizon, and the birds were up and chattering to each other. As Robinson and I walked down the leafy streets, I felt the neighborhood stirring. What if some guy stepped outside to grab the newspaper and saw us, two truants, suspiciously inspecting the neighborhood cars?

"Come on, Robinson," I said. "Let's get out of here." I was still hoping we'd make the bus. We had ten minutes left.

"I just want the perfect thing," he said.

At that moment, we saw a flash in the corner of our eyes. It was white and fast and coming toward us. I gasped and reached out for Robinson.

He laughed and pulled me close. "Whoa, Axi, get a grip. It's only a dog."

My heart was thrumming. "Yeah, I can see that...now."

I could also now see it wasn't likely to be an attack dog, either. He was a small thing, with short, patchy fur. No collar, no tags. I took a step forward, my hand extended, and the dog flinched. He turned around and went right up to Robinson instead (of course) and licked his hand. Then the darn thing lay down at his feet. Robinson knelt to pet him.

"Robinson," I said, getting impatient, "Greyhound bus or stolen car, the time is now."

He didn't seem to hear me. His long, graceful hands gently tugged on the dog's ears, and the dog rolled onto his side. As Robinson scratched the dog's belly, the animal's leg twitched and his pink tongue lolled out of his little mouth in total canine ecstasy.

"You're such a good boy," Robinson said gently. "Where do you belong?"

Even though the dog couldn't answer, we knew. He was skinny and his fur was clumped with mud. There was a patch of raw bare skin on his back. This dog was no one's dog.

"I wish you could come with us," Robinson said. "But we have a long way to go, and I don't think you'd dig it."

The dog looked at him like he'd dig anything in the world

as long as it involved more petting by Robinson. But when you're running away from your life and you can't take anything you don't need, a stray dog falls in the category of Not Necessary.

"Give him a little love, Axi," Robinson urged.

I bent down and dug my fingers into the dog's dirty coat the way I'd seen Robinson do, and when I ran my hand down the dog's chest, I could feel the quick flutter of his heart, the excitement of finding a home, someone to care for him.

Poor thing, I thought. Somehow, I knew exactly what he was feeling. He had no one, and he was stuck here.

But we weren't. Not anymore.

"We're leaving, little buddy. I'm sorry," I said. "We've just got to go."

It was totally weird, but for some reason that good-bye hurt almost as much as the one I'd whispered to my father.

4

WE LEFT THE DOG WITH ONE OF
Robinson's sticks of beef jerky, then headed to the end of the
block, where Robinson pulled up short. "There it is," he whispered, with real awe in his voice. He grabbed my hand and we
hurried through the intersection.

"There *what* is?" I asked, but of course he didn't answer me.

If things went on like this, we'd have to have a little talk—
because I didn't want a traveling companion who paid attention
to 50 percent of whatever came out of my mouth. If I wanted to
be ignored, I could just stay in Klamath Falls with my idiotic
classmates and my alcoholic father.

"There is the answer," Robinson said finally, sighing so big
you'd have thought he just fell in love. He turned to me and
bent down in an exaggerated bow, sweeping his arm out like a
valet at some superfancy restaurant (the kind of place we don't
have in K-Falls).

"Alexandra, milady, your chariot awaits," Robinson said with a wild grin. I rolled my eyes at him, like I always do when he does this fake-British shtick with my full name.

And then I rolled my eyes again: my so-called chariot, it turned out, was actually a *motorcycle*. A big black Harley-Davidson with yards of shining chrome, and two black leather side bags decorated with silver grommets. There were tassels on the handlebars and two cushioned seats. The thing gleamed like it was straight off the showroom floor.

Robinson was beside me, whispering in some foreign language. "Twin Cam Ninety-Six V-Twin," he said, then something about "electronic throttle control and six-speed transmission" and then a bunch of other things I didn't understand.

It was an amazing bike, even I could see that, and I can hardly tell a dirt bike from a Ducati. "Awesome," I said, checking my watch. "But we *really* should keep moving."

That was when I realized Robinson was bending toward the thing with a screwdriver in his hand.

"Are you out of your *mind*?" I hissed.

But Robinson didn't answer me. Again.

He was going to *hot-wire* the thing. *Holy s—*

I ran to the other side of the street and ducked down between two cars. Adrenaline rushed through my veins and I pressed my eyes shut.

There was no way this was happening, I told myself. No way he was going to actually get the thing started, no way this was how our journey would begin.

28

I had it all planned out, and it looked nothing like this.

Then the roar of an engine split open the quiet morning. I opened my eyes and a second later Robinson's feet appeared, one on either side of the Harley.

We're breaking the law! I should have screamed. But my mind simply couldn't process this change in plans. I couldn't say anything at all. I just thought: *He's running away in cowboy boots! That is so not practical!* And: *Why didn't I bring mine?*

"Stand up, Axi," Robinson yelled. "Get on."

I was rooted to the spot, my chest tight with anxiety. I was going to have a heart attack right here on Cedar Street, in between a pickup and a Volvo with a MY OTHER CAR IS A BROOM bumper sticker. So much for my great escape!

But then Robinson reached down and hauled me up, and the next thing I knew I was sitting behind him on the throbbing machine with the engine revving.

"Put your arms around me," he yelled.

I was so heart-and-soul terrified that I did.

"Now hang on!"

He put the thing in gear and we took off, the engine thundering in my ears. My dad was probably going to wake up on the couch and wonder if he'd just heard the rumble of an early-summer storm.

We shot past the Safeway, past the high school football field, past the Reel M Inn Tavern, where every Friday night my dad hooked himself up to a Budweiser IV, and past the "Mexican" restaurant (where they put Parmesan cheese on top of their burritos).

Yeah, Klamath Falls. It was the kind of place that looked best in a rearview mirror.

Seeing it flash past me, feeling the rush of the wind in my face, I suddenly didn't care if we woke up the entire stinking town.

Eat my dust! I wanted to shout.

Robinson let out a joyful whoop.

We'd done it. We were free.

5

THIS WASN'T ANYTHING LIKE THE MOPED
I rode once. It wasn't like anything I'd ever felt before. We
weren't even on the highway yet, but already it felt like we were
flying.

Then above the roar of the engine I heard Robinson's
voice. *"I don't want a tickle / 'Cause I'd rather ride on my motor-
sickle!"* It was an old Arlo Guthrie song. I knew the words because
my dad used to sing them to me when I was a little girl.

*"And I don't want to diiiiie / Just want to ride on my motorcy…
cle,"* I joined in, even though I can't carry a tune to save my life.

Robinson leisurely steered us past strip malls on the out-
skirts of town. He was whistling now (because if you ever want
to blow out your vocal cords, try singing loudly enough to be
heard over a Harley). He was acting like it was no big deal to
be zipping away on a stolen motorcycle.

My God, what in the world did we think we were doing? We were supposed to be on a bus, and instead we were on a stolen motorcycle that cost more than my dad made in two years. Escape was one thing, but robbery took it to another level. Suddenly I couldn't stop picturing the disappointment on my dad's face when he posted my bail, or the headline in the *Klamath Falls Herald and News*—GOOD GIRL GONE BAD—next to an unflattering mug shot that washed out my blue eyes and pale skin.

I tried not to imagine a cop around every bend as we headed south of the Klamath Falls Country Club, where my mom used to go for sloe gin fizzes on Ladies' Poker Night. And I kind of freaked out when we were actually acknowledged by another motorcycle rider, heading into town. As he passed, the biker dropped his arm down, two fingers angling toward the road, and Robinson mirrored the gesture.

"Don't take your hands off the handlebars!" I yelled. "Ever!"

"But it's the Harley wave," Robinson hollered.

"So?"

"So it's rude not to do it back!"

Of course, manners are useless when you're flat on your back in the bottom of a ditch....I didn't say that to Robinson, though, because I had to admit, Robinson was driving the motorcycle like he'd done it a thousand times before. Had he? Didn't a person need a special license to drive a motorcycle? And what about the hot-wiring? It would've taken me that long to figure out how to start the motorcycle with a key. Yeah, we had a few things to talk about, Robinson and me.

Past the Home Depot and Eddie's 90-Days-Same-as-Cash, Robinson yelled something, but the roar of the engine swallowed his voice. I think it was "Are you ready?" I didn't know what he was talking about, but whatever it was, I was probably *not* ready. Then I noticed that the speed limit went up to fifty-five, and Robinson pulled back on the throttle.

This may be obvious, but the thing about being on a motorcycle is that there is nothing between you and the world. (Or between you and the hard pavement.) The wind roars in your face. The sun shines in your eyes like a klieg light. There is no windshield. There are no seat belts. We were

going sixty-five now, and the little white needle was rising. I tightened my arms around Robinson's waist.

"What are you doing?" I yelled.

Eighty, and the roar of the wind drowned out the sound of my screaming.

Ninety, and tears were streaming from my eyes. I clung to Robinson for dear life.

One hundred, and I might as well have been on a rocket ship blasting into the stratosphere.

Adrenaline coursed through us like liquid fire. We were charged. Dangerous. The motorcycle shuddered and gained even more speed, and the wind was like a giant's merciless hand trying to push me off the back of the bike.

My life flashed before my eyes—my small, sad life.

Good riddance!

The fear was electrifying. It was terrifying and amazing, and if I'd thought I was having a heart attack before, I was *definitely* having one now.

And I was totally, dizzyingly, thrillingly loving every second of it.

In those brief moments, I shed my small-town good-girl reputation like an ugly sweater, and I burned it in the flames of the Harley insignia. We were runaways. Outlaws. Me and Robinson. Robinson and me.

And if we died in a fiery crash—well, we'd die happy, wouldn't we?

6

BUT WHETHER IT WAS LUCK OR FATE or Robinson's driving skills, we didn't die. We rode for hours along twisting back roads, until I felt like I'd molded myself to Robinson's back. Like I'd become some kind of giant girl-barnacle he'd need to pry off with that screwdriver of his.

At lunchtime we finally stopped in the town of Mount Shasta, California. It was tucked into the lower slope of a mountain, a giant, snow-streaked peak that's supposedly some kind of cosmic power center.

Yeah, you heard me right.

If you believe local legend, it's home to an ancient race of superhumans called Lemurians, who live in underground tunnels but surface every once in a while, seven feet tall and decked out in white robes. In other words, Mount Shasta is totally unlike Klamath Falls, which is the world's capital of monotony and is home to guys with names like Critter and Duke.

Also, UFOs have allegedly landed on Mount Shasta. And that's just the tip of the bizarro iceberg.

Even the smiling attendant at the Shell station was wearing a giant amethyst crystal around his neck and had a chakra diagram on his T-shirt.

Robinson returned the attendant's blissed-out grin, but his didn't come from Mount Shasta's cosmic power rays. It came from the Harley. He struck a pose, one hand on the gas tank, a thumb hooked in his belt loop, and offered me a goofy Hollywood sneer. "Am I James Dean or what? *Rebel Without a Cause?*"

I squinted at him. Though I would never admit it, Robinson kind of looked like he could be a movie star. Sure, he was a little on the skinny side, but that face of his? It belonged on a poster tacked to a teenybopper girl's bedroom wall.

"James Dean died in a car crash. You know, because he was *speeding*," I said. My legs were trembling so much I could barely stand. The thundering rumble of the engine had burrowed into my bones.

"I only sped once," Robinson countered. "I had to see what this bad boy could do."

"Once was plenty," I shot back, trying to sound stern. I'd loved it, sure. Because *ohmygod* it felt like flying. But I was pretty sure that—like paragliding or jumping out of an airplane—going 110 on the back of a stolen Harley was the sort of thing you only needed to do once.

Robinson walked into the station to pay for the gas and emerged with two coffees and a Slim Jim, which, if you ask me, is like eating a pepperoni-flavored garden hose. But Robinson had loved horrible food for as long as I'd known him.

We took a little stroll into the town center. There was a guy wearing a sandwich board that read ARE YOU SAVED? But instead of a picture of Jesus or angels, there was a drawing of a green-skinned alien holding up two fingers in a peace sign. Robinson stopped to talk to him. Of course.

I ducked into a health food store that smelled like patchouli and nutritional yeast and got some vegetables for our dinner. When I came outside, Robinson was reading a flyer that the man had given him.

"We could go on a spirit quest," he said. "Meet our Star Elders."

"No way, Scalawag," I said, snatching the pamphlet from

him and tossing it into a recycling bin. "As fascinating as that sounds, I spent months planning this trip, and last I checked, communing with our so-called Star Elders was not on the to-do list."

"Well, neither was stealing a motorcycle, and look how well that turned out."

He looked pretty proud of himself for that comeback.

"Okay, fine," I acknowledged. "It's been great so far. But we can't ride a hot bike across the country. For one thing, we'll get caught. And for another, I don't think my butt can take it."

Robinson laughed. "You actually look kind of annoyed right now. Are you?"

"No," I lied. "But next time, *I* pick the ride."

"Oh, Axi—" he began.

"I don't want this trip to be a huge mistake, okay?" I interrupted. "I'm not interested in jail time."

Robinson leaned over and plucked a faceted glass orb from the sidewalk display in front of the Soul Connections gift shop. He waved it in front of my face. "By everything that is cosmic and weird and awesome, I banish all doubts from your mind." He glanced at the price tag. "Only five ninety-five. A bargain!"

He dashed into the store and a moment later reappeared with the orb nestled in a purple velvet bag. He placed it in my hands. "This is magic," he said. "It will keep you from ever being annoyed at me again."

"Don't count on it," I said drily. But I couldn't help smiling at him. "Thanks. It's really pretty."

"Axi," Robinson said, his voice softer now, "if this trip is a mistake, it's the best one we'll ever make."

And somehow, by the look he gave me then, I knew he was right.

7

BY THE TIME WE STOPPED AT A CAMP-
ground in Humboldt Redwoods State Park, we'd been driving
for seven hours. Robinson had stuck to the back roads, and
I wasn't complaining. My fear of getting pulled over by
cops looking for a black Harley with an Oregon plate hadn't
completely disappeared, but I was thinking about it less as we
got farther and farther from home.

The sun was low above the horizon when we pulled into
the park, and it vanished completely as we entered the green
canopy of trees. Robinson let out a low whistle as the shadows
enveloped us.

Old-growth redwoods. How can I even describe them?
They towered above us darkly, and they felt *alive*. Not alive like
regular trees, but alive like they had souls. Like they were wise,
ancient creatures, watching with only the faintest hint of interest as two road-weary teenagers walked beneath them. The air

was cool and slightly damp, and the silence was profound. I felt like we were in church.

"I totally understand the whole Druid thing now," Robinson whispered.

"I think the Druids actually worshipped oak trees," I noted. "They didn't have redwoods in ancient Ireland."

"Smarty-pants," Robinson said, poking me.

I put my hand on a rough, cool trunk. "Majestic tranquility," I said softly, seeing how the words felt in my mouth. A little too pretentious: I wouldn't be writing that down in my journal. But there were *real* writers who'd seen redwoods like these, and I could steal from them, couldn't I? "'They are not like any trees we know, they are ambassadors from another time,'" I said.

"Huh?" said Robinson.

"John Steinbeck wrote that in *Travels with Charley.*"

He sighed. "Another one of the books you gave me—"

"That you didn't read."

Robinson used to pretend he felt guilty about ignoring the stacks of books I passed him, but eventually he stopped bothering. "I thought I was supposed to read *East of Eden* first," he said.

"Let me know when you get to it," I said. "I won't hold my breath."

"Well, you can let me know when you listen to that Will Oldham CD I got you."

"I put it on my iPod but, as you know, it's broken," I pointed out. "Your eyeballs work just fine."

We found our campsite then, a small clearing surrounded by a ring of redwoods, with a picnic bench, a fire pit, and a spigot for cold, clear water. I unhooked my tent from the backpack. It was an army-green miracle of engineering: big enough to contain two people and their sleeping bags, it weighed less than a pound and, folded up, fit into a bag the size of a loaf of Wonder Bread. Robinson eyed it, impressed.

"Watch how I set this up," I directed. "Because tomorrow night it's your job."

"I thought it was the woman's job to keep house and the man's job to hunt for food," he said, grinning slyly.

I snorted. "Are you planning to kill an elk with your screwdriver? Good luck."

"I was thinking more along the lines of a squirrel," he said, but even that was ridiculous, because Robinson would never hurt anything. I mean, the guy had to grit his teeth to kill a mosquito.

I unpacked the veggies I'd bought, plus a hunk of aged Gouda and a bag of lavash, the thin flatbread I love and couldn't get in Klamath Falls because apparently it was too *exotic*.

"Well, well, well," Robinson said as he watched me skewer mushrooms and peppers on sticks I'd stripped of their bark. "I guess you'd do all right on *Survivor*."

I rolled my eyes at him. "I paid for this stuff, Robinson. I didn't forage for wild green peppers and cheese. Now, are you going to gather some sticks for the fire or what?"

"You couldn't buy firewood, too?" he asked, but he ambled good-naturedly into the brush to find things to burn.

Soon we had a nice fire going, and we roasted our kebabs over the flickering flames. I stuck slices of cheese between pieces of lavash, wrapped them in foil, and set them near the fire until the cheese melted. When everything was ready, we leaned against a fallen log that was covered with springy green moss, which made a surprisingly comfortable backrest. We didn't have plates, and the vegetables were a bit burned in places, but it was the best dinner I'd ever had. It tasted like freedom.

Robinson complimented my cooking, but within the hour he was raiding my backpack for junk food, claiming to be suffering from vitamin overdose.

"What else do you have in here?" he demanded. "I know

you're keeping Fritos or Oreos or something terrible and delicious from me." I watched as he pulled out the map, two featherlight rain ponchos, my Dr. Bronner's, my toothbrush, and my journal.

"Open that on pain of death," I warned.

Finally Robinson held up a chocolate bar, triumphant.

"Half for you, half for me," he said.

"A *quarter* for you and a *quarter* for me," I corrected. "I'm rationing."

Robinson laughed. "You're a planner, I know. You always have everything figured out. But do you really think there's a shortage of chocolate bars on the West Coast?" He reached out and handed me a small piece of chocolate. When our fingertips touched, I twitched as if I'd been shocked. It surprised both of us.

"You're jittery all of a sudden," he said. "We're safe here, Axi. No one's going to find us." He walked over to the bike and lovingly patted its seat. "Or the hot Harley."

While Robinson fondled his new toy, I tried to calm down, breathing in that "sweeter, rarer, healthier air," as old Walt Whitman would say. Night was coming, bringing darkness and deeper silence. It seemed like in all the world, there were only the two of us.

I'd always told Robinson pretty much everything I thought about, but I couldn't tell him this: I wasn't nervous about being discovered. I was suddenly nervous about something else.

Sleeping arrangements.

8

INSIDE THE TENT, I UNROLLED OUR sleeping bags. There wasn't an inch to spare. We were going be *thisclose* to each other, Robinson and me.

He was still outside the tent, throwing leaves into the fire and watching them curl and blacken. "Do we need to string up the packs? You know, to protect them from bears?" he called.

"There aren't any bears around here," I assured him, smoothing out my bag. It was pink camo. Hideously ugly, but it'd been on sale. "Only elk. Spotted owls. That sort of thing."

Robinson poked his head inside the tent. "Do you know that for real?" he asked. "Or are you just saying it to make yourself feel better?" He looked me right in the eyes. He knew me too well.

"I'm, like, sixty percent positive," I admitted. "Or less."

Robinson was unsurprised. "I'm stringing up the packs, then."

He ducked back out and I heard him rustling around. He

took a long time, whether because he was new to the demands of camping or because he was sneaking more of the chocolate bar…well, that could be his secret.

When he popped his head in again, he was grinning. There was a tiny spot of melted chocolate in the corner of his mouth. "Cozy in here, isn't it?"

Then he slipped off his boots and climbed all the way inside, and cozy became something of an understatement. I felt weirdly shy. Like suddenly my body was bigger and more awkward—and more *female*—than it had ever been before. I wondered if I smelled like motor oil and BO. I noticed that Robinson smelled like campfire, like soap, like *boy*.

Robinson could have had his pick of girls from our high school. Even after he dropped out (which for everyone else who'd done it was the social kiss of death), all the cheerleaders and the student council girls still wanted to take him to prom. Sometimes I pictured them hanging off his arms, like those little game pieces in Barrel of Monkeys, brightly colored and plastic.

"I'm not interested in them," he'd say. Eventually, I'd gotten up the nerve to ask: who—or what—was he interested in? He'd laughed and slung his arm around my shoulders the way he did sometimes.

"I'm interested in you, GG," he'd said lightly. As if that settled it.

But what did that mean, really? Because as far as I could tell, he wasn't interested in me in *that* way. We'd held hands a few times, like when we were in the movie theater watching *Cabin in the Woods* or *Paranormal Activity*. And once when I'd drunk three-quarters of a beer, I had kissed him, sloppily, good night.

But that was all, folks.

Now we lay side by side, staring at the tent ceiling only three feet above our heads. I listened to the wind in the tops of the trees and the sound of Robinson's breathing, and for the first time considered what traveling together would mean in practical terms. Where was I supposed to change? What if I wanted to sleep in my underwear? What would Robinson think when he saw me in the morning, mussed and sleepy, with tousled hair and flushed cheeks and breath that could kill a small animal?

Not that that was the problem. No, the problem—or, at the very least, the Thing That Mattered—was that we would be sleeping right next to each other. Alone. Not even a stuffed teddy bear between us.

Robinson shifted, trying to make himself comfortable. No doubt he was realizing the same thing I was. I cleared my throat.

"Before you say anything," Robinson said, "here's the deal."

I could almost hear my heart doing a tiny shuffling dance.

"Stealing is—well, it's not a good thing, Axi, but it's not necessarily that bad, either. I mean, we're taking good care of the bike. And this guy's going to get it back."

That dancing ticker of mine slowed. I'd thought we were going to talk about *us*. Honestly, I was already over the stealing.

Regret is a waste of time, my mom used to say. She'd served up that platitude a lot before she split town. Maybe it made her feel better about leaving.

"And if for some reason he doesn't get it back," Robinson went on, "his insurance covers the loss and he gets a brand-new one."

He made it sound so simple. And maybe it was. In some ways it was simpler than talking about *us*.

Robinson rolled over so he was facing me. His nose, I noticed, was sunburned. His chin was covered in faint dark stubble. I watched his Adam's apple move as he swallowed. Our eyes met, but I quickly looked away.

He reached out and brushed a piece of hair from my forehead. I held my breath.

Suddenly I understood that running away was all the thrill I could stand today. If Robinson touched any other part of me, I might explode into a million pieces.

But he didn't touch me again. He smiled. "Sweet dreams, Axi Moore," he said softly. Then he rolled back over.

Inside I ached a little, but I wasn't sure what for.

9

I STARED INTO THE DARKNESS FOR A long time, feeling the contrast between the cold, hard ground beneath me and the soft warmth of Robinson beside me. Thoughts raced through my mind endlessly: *What if Robinson and I get caught? Or if we chicken out and go back home? Or if we keep on and each night lie side by side, chaste as children? If we kiss? If we whisper the word* love, *or if it remains unsaid forever?*

It would probably only matter to me. I didn't know if it would matter to Robinson. I tentatively put my head on his shoulder, but he didn't move a muscle.

When I finally slept, I dreamed we were on the edge of a cliff, peering down. Dream-Robinson was holding my hand. "Don't worry," he said. "It only looks like a cliff. It's actually a mountain, and the way is up, not down."

Even in dreams, he was an optimist.

By the time Robinson stumbled out of the tent the next morning, looking rumpled and adorable, I'd packed our bags and plotted our route to Bolinas, a tiny town nestled between the California hills and the Pacific Ocean. I wanted to see it mostly because the town is supposed to be a secret. The people who live there are always tearing down the road signs that point to it. But that wasn't going to stop me from discovering what the big deal was about this place.

"Maybe," Robinson said teasingly as he mounted the bike, "buried deep inside the Good Girl, there's the heart of a rebel."

"Haven't I already proven that to you by suggesting this crazy trip?" I climbed up behind him and commanded, "Now, *drive*."

Naturally, we missed our turn the first time, but when we finally got there, we were a little mystified.

"*This* is what they want to keep to themselves?" Robinson asked.

The downtown consisted of two intersecting streets. There was a restaurant called the Coast Café—which, FYI, did not overlook the coast—and an old-fashioned-looking bar. I had to agree: Bolinas didn't seem particularly inspiring.

But the adjacent beach was beautiful. We kicked our shoes off and sat down in the sand, staring at the blue water and feeling the sun on our shoulders. Tanned, half-wild children ran around us, throwing rocks at seagulls. Robinson started digging his toes in the sand, and more than once I caught him looking at me, an unreadable expression on his face.

"So...what are you thinking about?" I finally asked. I hoped he didn't detect the slight edge of apprehension in my question.

"Corn dogs," Robinson answered without missing a beat.

Sometimes I could just kill him.

He could have been thinking about me, about *us*, but instead his mind had settled on wieners encased in corn batter.

We ducked into Smiley's Schooner Saloon, and Robinson walked up to the bar like it was the counter at Ernie's. "Good afternoon, sir," he said. "Two Rainiers, please, and a corn dog."

I swear, if Robinson ever had to pick a last meal, it'd be corn dogs, French fries, and a deep-fried Twinkie.

"ID?" the bartender said.

Robinson fished out his wallet. The bartender's eyes darted from Robinson's fake license to Robinson's face and back again. "Okay... *Ned Dixon*." Then he turned to me.

I shrugged. "I wasn't driving, see, so I left my license back—"

The bartender crossed his meaty arms. "Listen, *kids*, how about you head across the street and get yourself a nice ice-cream cone at the café."

"Actually, I'm lactose intol—" Robinson began, but I interrupted him.

"Oh, *I* get it!" My voice came out surprisingly fierce. "We can fight in Afghanistan, but we can't have a beer and watch the sunset?" My hands gripped the edge of the bar and I leaned forward, hostility coming off me in waves. I had no idea where this was coming from, but it actually felt kind of good to be angry with someone. Someone who didn't matter, someone I would never see again.

I probably would have yelled more, but Robinson dragged me outside. Then he bent over, practically choking with laughter. "Fight in Afghanistan?" he wheezed. "Us?"

"It just came out," I said, still not sure what had just happened. I started to giggle a little, too.

Robinson wiped his eyes. "You don't even like beer."

"It was a matter of principle. A lot of people die in Afghanistan before they're allowed to buy a six-pack."

"A lot of people die every day, Axi. They don't go off on bartenders in secret towns about the unfairness of the drinking laws. I can't wait to see what you come up with next," he said, still laughing at my outburst as he strode ahead of me.

His flip tone made me stop short in the middle of the sidewalk. Yeah, people *do* die every day. Some people, like Carole Ann, die before they even learn to tie their shoes. Others die before they graduate from high school.

Hell, either one of us could die on this crazy trip.

There were so many more important things to do than buy a beer before that happened. I hurried to catch up with Robinson, who was turning the corner to where we'd parked the motorcycle in an empty lot behind the saloon. But now there was a man in a leather jacket and chaps standing right beside it, giving it a long—and much-too-close-for-my-comfort—look.

"Nice bike," the guy said. "Got a cousin in Oregon who has one exactly like it."

My lungs felt like bellows that someone had just squeezed shut. I took a step backward. Should we just run?

But Robinson didn't flinch. "Your cousin has good taste," he said. He glanced at the bike behind Chaps. "You riding a Fat Boy these days? I love those, but my girl here likes a bigger bike." His voice had taken on an easy drawl, like he and Chaps were two dudes who'd see eye to eye over a Harley.

Chaps was still sizing Robinson up: Robinson was taller but about a hundred pounds lighter. Me, I was still thinking

about running—and about how Robinson had called me his girl. That sounded…interesting. But did he mean it, or was it just part of his act?

"Happy hour's almost over, y'know," Robinson said.

Chaps gave him one long, last look, then shook his head and went inside.

I was already reaching for paper and pen.

Thanks so much for letting us ride your motorcycle, I wrote. *We took really good care of it. We named it Charley.*

Robinson read over my shoulder. "We did?"

"Just now," I said. "Charley the Harley."

I'm sorry we didn't ask you if we could borrow it, but rest assured that your bike was used only for the forces of good. Sincerely, GG & the Scalawag

I tucked the note into the handlebars. "Come on. Time to find another ride," I said, like I'd been stealing cars my whole life. In all of downtown Bolinas there were only about five cars, though.

"That one," I said, pointing to a silver Pontiac.

Robinson nodded. "Dead boring," he said. "But sensible."

I could feel the tingling beginning in my limbs. Robinson took a quick look around and then got in. I ducked into the passenger side, mentally thanking the owner for leaving the doors unlocked.

From his backpack Robinson removed a small cordless drill and aimed it at the keyhole. I watched as glittering flecks of metal fell onto the seat.

He packed a drill? I thought.

A grizzled surfer was looking right at us. I smiled and waved.

"Hurry up," I hissed at Robinson.

He produced his screwdriver and inserted it into the mangled keyhole. "One more minute."

The adrenaline tingle was growing more intense. Painful, even.

"I had to break the lock pins," Robinson explained.

As if I cared! I just wanted the engine to turn on. I sucked in a deep breath. Any moment we were going to be racing out of town, and everything would return to normal—my *new* normal, that is.

That was when two people came out of the Coast Café—and began heading toward their silver Pontiac. I met the woman's eyes, saw her jaw drop open. The man started running. "Hey," he shouted. *"Hey!"*

His arms flew forward, and he was just inches from us when the engine suddenly roared to life. Robinson slammed the car into reverse and we shot backward into the street. A moment later we were blazing out of town, going fifty in a twenty-five zone.

"I'm going to miss Charley," I said, my heart pounding.

Robinson nodded. "Me too."

"But not Bolinas," I added.

"That was *your* idea," Robinson reminded me with a smirk.

I shrugged and let out a deep sigh of relief. The sun was flashing deep vermilion over the blue ocean, calming me as I watched it slip lower and then vanish before my heart rate had even returned to normal.

Amazing how beauty can be so fleeting.

10

WE DROVE ACROSS THE GOLDEN GATE
Bridge that night, gliding over a dark San Francisco Bay into
the narrow streets of the Presidio. Since the car offered a solid
roof over our heads—and since cops apparently frown on urban
camping—we decided to spend the night in the Pontiac.

I curled up in the backseat, and Robinson folded himself,
with difficulty, into the front. There was no question of us
touching (or, as the case may be, not touching) with all that
upholstery in the way. A tiny part of me felt relieved, but a
larger part of me longed for the so-cozy-it's-claustrophobic
tent.

That was my realization for the night: I was capable of missing Robinson when he was less than two feet away from me.

I was starting to develop a theory about missing things in
general. It had started when we left Charley the Harley behind,

and I hadn't stopped thinking about it the rest of the drive. If I practiced missing small things—like the rumbling ride of a motorcycle, or the faint murmur of my dad talking in his sleep, or now sleeping right next to Robinson—maybe I could get used to missing things. Then, when it came time to miss something really important, maybe I could survive it.

We listened to the radio for a while, Robinson humming along and me keeping my tuneless mouth shut until we drifted off. In the morning, fog rolling in from the bay blurred the streetlights into soft orange halos. I peered over the seat at Robinson's tangled limbs.

"Rise and shine," I sang. He opened one eye and gave me the finger.

Not everyone is a morning person.

"There's someone I want you to meet," I told him.

"Now?" Robinson asked. But I simply handed him his shoes.

There was one book I'd gotten Robinson to read in the last six months. *The Winding Road* was a memoir about growing up as the daughter of an alcoholic father (I could seriously relate) and a beauty-queen mother (ditto) in a small town in southern Oregon. The author, Matthea North, could have been me, which is maybe why I found her story so fascinating. A couple of years ago, I wrote her a fan letter. She wrote me back, and an epistolary friendship—I guess you could call it that—was born.

(*Epistolary*: a word I'm not going to use in front of Robinson.)

You must stop by for a visit some time, Matthea had written. *We'll drink tea and ponder the vagaries of love, the secrets of life, the mysteries of the universe...*

If ever there was a time for that conversation, it was now.

Matthea's house was on Nob Hill, at the top of an impossibly steep street. I rang the bell and we waited nervously on the stoop. Robinson didn't even know what we were doing here, and I refused to tell him. If you ask me, a person doesn't get enough good surprises in life. Birthday, Christmas...that's only two times a year to count on.

But when the front door opened, I was even more surprised than Robinson. Since Matthea North and I had so much in common childhood-wise, I guess I thought she'd look like an older version of me: slender, medium-sized, with the full lips and wide-set eyes of a beauty-queen mother somehow diluted into a slightly less remarkable prettiness.

Matthea looked like Bilbo Baggins. In a Gypsy costume. Under five feet tall, bedecked in scarves and necklaces, she reached up to take my hand. "You must be Axi," she said. Her green eyes, set deep in rosy cheeks, positively twinkled at me.

I swallowed. "Yes!" I said brightly. "Robinson, this is...the one and only Matthea North."

He turned toward her, smiling his wide, gorgeous grin. "Hey, you wrote that book—the one about the town even worse than ours." If he was fazed by her clothes, he didn't look it.

Matthea laughed. Older ladies love Robinson.

We followed her into the darkness of her home, and already she was chattering about how Mark Twain never said the famous line about how the coldest winter he ever spent was a summer in San Francisco, but he should have, because it was absolutely Arctic today; how birdsong had evolved over decades to compete with the sound of traffic, and weren't those sparrows outside just deafeningly loud; how she'd gotten a bad fortune in her cookie from Lucky Feng's, but did we know that it was the Japanese who'd actually invented the fortune cookie?

She motioned for us to sit on a dusty-looking Victorian couch. "I loved your short story about that old deli, Axi," she said, "the one about that girl and boy who are best friends but maybe something more—"

"Oh, yeah, thanks," I said hurriedly, not wanting to cut her off but needing to.

Robinson cleared his throat. I could practically hear him thinking: *You wrote a story about Ernie's? And us?*

I ignored him. Of course I'd written about him. He was my best friend, wasn't he? The one who knew me like no other. The one I thought about approximately 75 percent of my waking hours, if not more.

"Thanks for letting us come over," I said. "I really wanted Robinson to meet you. I can't get him to finish any book, ever, but he read yours in a night."

"It gave me...insights," Robinson said, looking pointedly at me.

Matthea laughed. "Axi and I share certain background details, don't we? But Axi's much smarter than I was at her age."

"She's ornerier," Robinson said. "That's for sure."

I kicked him in the shins—lightly.

Matthea produced a pitcher of iced tea and a plate of sugar cookies, and Robinson helped himself to two.

"So, how's the writing going, Axi?" Matthea asked.

"Um, not much at all lately," I admitted, reaching for my own cookie. "Please tell me there's some secret to keeping at it. Not giving up. Believing in yourself. That kind of stuff." I tried to keep the desperation out of my voice.

Matthea sighed and began to braid the fringe on her scarf. "My dear, there is no universal secret. There's only the secret each writer discovers for herself. The path forward."

I could feel my shoulders slump. Of course. There's no such thing as a magic bullet. Who doesn't know that?

"Are you aware that European kings used to have their hearts buried separately from their bodies?" Matthea asked.

"Um...no," I said, and I saw Robinson raise his eyebrows with that slight grin I loved. Clearly, he was amused by my weirdo writing mentor.

"It was a way of offering their hearts, literally and figuratively, to their country. Forever." Matthea sighed. "Macabre practice, if you ask me. But I like it as a metaphor. You

give your country—which, in this case, is your story—your heart."

"Oh," I said. "Okay." No wonder I hadn't written the Great American Novel yet. My heart was still firmly planted in my chest. Wasn't it?

"Be patient," Matthea said gently. "Keep writing, but keep dreaming, too. Remember that inspiration struck the brilliant mathematician Archimedes when he was in the bathtub."

And inspiration struck the brilliant physicist Richard Feynman when he was in a strip club, I thought. (I may be failing AP physics, but I did learn a thing or two.)

That's pretty much how the rest of the conversation went. We didn't ponder the unpredictability of love or the mysteries of the universe, but since we touched on everything from the mummified hearts of European kings to Einstein's theory that creativity was more important than knowledge, I felt like it was time well spent.

After a fourth sugar cookie, though, Robinson excused himself, saying he needed to get a bit of fresh air. I watched his retreating back, feeling a vague sense of unease. My body gave an involuntary shiver, and Matthea looked at me piercingly. We continued our chat, but later, as we were leaving, she put her hand on my shoulder. "Are you all right?" she asked.

For one tiny millisecond, I wanted to tell her everything. The real reason behind what Robinson and I were doing, which I hadn't even wanted to admit to myself this whole time. It didn't actually have anything to do with me escaping my boring life in Klamath Falls. But I couldn't tell her.

"I'm great," I said.

"And your friend?" She squinted toward Robinson, who was leaning against the car, staring down the hill toward the bay. He brought his arms up and almost seemed to hug himself, as if he were cold. Or as if, for a moment, he felt the need to reassure himself about something.

"He's great, too," I insisted. *Why are you lying, Axi?*

Matthea picked a yellow flower from one of the vines around her door and tucked it behind my ear. "Give your story your heart," she repeated.

It sounded reasonable enough. But when I looked at Robinson, I knew I'd already given my heart to something—to someone—else.

11

IF I DIDN'T KNOW IT WAS MEDICALLY impossible, I'd say that Robinson was born with a wrench in his hand. Or that as a baby, he sucked on a spark plug instead of a pacifier.

This gearhead gene was why I was taking him to Torrance, California, next—because it certainly wasn't my kind of place. Torrance breeds NASCAR drivers and semiprofessional cage fighters. (Ugh.) It has a racetrack, a giant rock 'n' roll car show, and about five hundred stores that sell car parts.

In other words, for a guy like Robinson, it's the Promised Land. The kind of place he had to—he *deserved* to—experience.

When we pulled into the parking lot of the Cal-Am Speedway the following afternoon, Robinson sucked in his breath and gave me his crooked, perfect grin.

"Axi Moore," he said, "you are greatest person I have ever known."

"You just wait," I said, smiling back.

I steered him away from the glass atrium entrance and toward a side door propped open with a rolled-up copy of *Car and Driver*.

Brad Sewell was waiting for us in the pit. "Alexandra," he said, stepping forward to give me a bear hug. "Long time no see, kiddo."

Robinson clearly wanted to know how this beefy dude with a Dale Earnhardt tattoo and I were acquainted. But I simply said, "Robinson, this is Brad. Brad, this is my friend Robinson."

"Nice to meet ya," Brad said. "Let me walk you through a few things, and then we'll get you in the cockpit."

It was only then that Robinson understood what he was actually here for, and he looked like he might spontaneously combust from excitement.

He turned to me. "It's like *Say Anything*," he whispered.

We'd watched that old movie a hundred times. One of the best scenes is when the geeky main character takes his reluctant date, one of the Beautiful People, to an art museum after hours. He can do this because he's friends with the museum guard, and because he's hung a painting of the Beautiful Girl in one of the galleries.

Today was my museum moment for Robinson, but better. I'd bribed Brad with a chunk of my savings, and I'd shamelessly

66

pulled the "I knew you when our sisters were in the cancer ward" card.

Brad began talking gibberish to Robinson, something about "initial turn-in" and "apex of the curve" and "neutral throttle on the corner." But Robinson was nodding confidently, and then he was climbing into a flame-resistant Nomex suit, and Brad was fitting him with a radio helmet and snapping him into a five-point harness.

"Any fool can speed on the straightaway; it's the curves

that make a racer," Brad said over his shoulder.

"Oh, sure," I said. Like I knew what he was talking about—I couldn't even drive to the grocery store.

Robinson revved the engine and then pulled out of the pit. He didn't go that fast at first, but he must have gotten the hang of it after a while, because the engine got louder and the car became a green blur flashing past us again and again.

"So how's your little sister?" I asked Brad.

"She's in remission. Two years now."

"That's fantastic," I said. Lizzie Sewell had been really nice to Carole Ann. Lizzie, it seems, was one of the lucky ones.

"And what about you?" Brad asked, and I pretended not to hear. Fortunately, just at that moment, the bright green car came screeching to a halt on the track outside the pit, and Robinson opened the door.

"Axi, you have *got* to get in here!" he yelled.

I looked over at Brad. I was hoping he'd tell me that the other seat belt was broken or that he was fresh out of helmets.

"There's a suit over there that'll fit you," he said.

And that's how I found myself in the passenger seat of a custom Chevy race car, outfitted like Danica Patrick and quivering with excitement.

"On your mark, get set, go!" yelled Robinson, and we peeled out onto the track, zero to sixty in about a millisecond.

The g-force slammed me against the seat, and the stunning, brain-shaking roar of the engine filled my ears. I could feel the noise as much as hear it. It vibrated in my chest and shook me deep in my guts.

I couldn't help it: in joy and terror, I screamed.

I stopped, though, because I couldn't even hear myself. And then I screamed some more.

We came toward the first curve, and I noticed the tall wire fence that arced inward over the track. Somehow I understood—even though I was totally incapable of higher thought,

of abstract things such as words—that the fence was to keep us from splattering our body parts all over the bleachers in a crash.

The car had thick mesh netting instead of windows, so the wind came rushing in, hot and smelling like asphalt and oil. I couldn't see how fast we were going, and I didn't want to know.

We banked around the curve, the engine squealing.

As we pulled into the straightaway and Robinson hit hard on the throttle, suddenly my vision seemed to narrow. It was like looking through a tunnel. Everything on either side of

me blurred and faded, and all that mattered was the airspace in front of us, and how lightning fast we were going to blast through it.

My body was singing with fear and happiness and an incredible feeling of being completely alive in the moment. I was no longer Alexandra Jane Moore—I was a supernova strapped into a bucket seat.

Go, go, go! I thought wildly. Because screaming, after all, was useless.

We took three more sound barrier–shattering laps, and when we finally slowed, I turned to Robinson with wide and no doubt crazy-looking eyes.

"Oh my God," I said, pulling off my helmet and shaking out my sweat-drenched hair. "Oh. My. God."

Robinson cackled madly. Brad came over and said, "Whaddja think?"

It took Robinson a moment to answer, probably because he had to wait for his brain to stop vibrating. Then he said, "I might have just had the best time of my life."

I started laughing like an idiot, because that was exactly what we'd come for, what I'd wanted to give him.

Carpe diem. Because today, after all, was all we knew we had.

12

"I'M STANDING ON TOM CRUISE," Robinson yelled. "Take my picture!"

"You're on his *star*, Scalawag," I said. But I snapped the photo anyway: dark-eyed Robinson, handsome as any movie star, dressed like a hipster lumberjack. Even in Southern California, he couldn't give up the flannel.

We were fresh off the Cal-Am racetrack, still hopped up on the experience. Hollywood was a hop, skip, and a jump up the 110 from Torrance, so that's where we went next.

Of course we had to go straight to the Walk of Fame. While Robinson ogled the street performers (buskers, hustlers, and dudes dressed like Iron Man and Captain Jack Sparrow), I dashed around taking photos of the names I knew and loved: Marilyn Monroe, Audrey Hepburn, James

Dean...and, okay, Drew Barrymore and Jennifer Aniston, because it's the twenty-first century, people, and not all good movies are in black and white.

"This place is nuts," Robinson said, hopping over to Snow White's star. "Look, now I'm on top of a fairy tale."

"'I used to be Snow White, but I drifted,'" I said. Then I cocked a hip and gave my best sultry wink—like Mae West, whose line I'd just stolen.

Then I turned, and together we walked up Highland Avenue, toward the golden Hollywood Hills and the giant, iconic white sign. Our destination: the Hollywood Hotel. Robinson didn't know it, though, because I wanted to keep surprising him. The delight on his face—the way his eyes went wide when he was taken aback—I wanted to keep seeing that for as long as I possibly could.

The fact that we would be alone together in a hotel room had nothing to with my decision.

(Quit laughing!)

When Robinson saw me striding up to the reservation desk, he said, "Do we have enough money for this?"

I wasn't sure if we did, but it didn't matter. "My back can't take another night in the car, and I am *not* camping out with those shirtless dudes I saw in the park." (If I couldn't tell him the truth, didn't that seem like a good enough reason?)

"I thought that guy with the python looked nice," Robinson joked. "But hey, I'm down with creature comforts. Are we gonna get room service?"

I shook my head. "Nice try," I said. "Spendthrift. Profligate."

"I totally don't know what those words mean," Robinson said, "but I'm not the one who booked us the expensive hotel room."

We rode the mirrored elevator to the fifteenth floor in silence. We didn't meet each other's eyes, either in person or in our reflections. Did Robinson feel shy, the way I suddenly did? I didn't know, because I couldn't look at him.

A minute later, we opened a door onto a spacious cream-colored room, with a giant flat-screen TV, floor-to-ceiling windows, a little seating area, and one giant boat of a bed.

I felt my breath catch in my throat. Robinson and I had slept in a tent, as close together as spoons. And this bed was so stupidly huge that we could be on either side of it and not touch at all. And yet—it felt way more intimate.

I went to the sink to wash the racetrack grit from my face. In the mirror was a girl I hardly recognized. For one thing, she desperately needed a shower. For another, she looked…well, *wild* was the word that came to mind. Certainly she did not resemble a *straight arrow* or a *do-gooder,* which were the kinds of nouns I was used to.

I met her pale blue eyes and smiled faintly at her. *Who are you? What do you want?* I mouthed. But she only offered me that strange smirk.

When I came out of the bathroom, Robinson was already

in bed, though it was barely after eight. He was wearing an ancient Bob Dylan T-shirt and pressing buttons on the remote. The TV was on but muted.

"Axi Moore," he said, smiling at me, the blue light from the screen flickering on his handsome face.

"Robinson," I said, barely above a whisper.

"What do you want to do now?" he asked.

I almost cracked up. That was the question to end all

questions, wasn't it?

For a moment I stood there, caught between the hallway and the bed, between fear and desire. On the one hand, I wanted to sink into Robinson. Reach my fingers into his hair. Feel his lips on my neck. Hold his smooth skin close against mine.

But then I thought of the dream I'd had among the redwoods—how something could be both perfect and terrifying, both mountain and abyss. *What was the right thing to do?*

"Hey, look," Robinson said suddenly, his voice brightening. "It's *Puss in Boots.*"

Just like that, the tension in the air snapped. We loved that movie, even though it's for kids. Robinson insisted—I think seriously—that it was Antonio Banderas's best role.

So the fuzzy orange cat with the big boots and the Spanish accent banished my questions and doubts until another day. I crawled under the covers next to Robinson. The sheets were silky white and smelled like bleach. I took a deep breath, and I scooted right up against his side. Then I tipped my head onto his shoulder.

Robinson seemed to stiffen. I froze, too. My heart sank in my chest, and my eyes closed in shame. Had I read the situation so wrong? I told myself I would count to five and then pull away to the far side of the giant bed.

But then I felt Robinson's body shift. He curved toward

me. And he leaned down and kissed the top of my head. Under the covers, his hand found mine. Our fingers intertwined.

That's enough, I thought. *That's all I need.*

For now.

13

OVER BREAKFAST THE NEXT MORNING, Robinson told me he had something to confess.

We were in Starbucks, eating microwaved Artisan Breakfast Sandwiches, which, FYI, have nothing artisanal about them. At the table next to us, a Stormtrooper and an unconvincing Michael Jackson sipped Venti dark roasts before taking up their posts along the Walk of Fame.

"Spill it," I said. I felt a slight fluttering beneath my rib cage. *He's going to say he's sorry, that he should have kissed me last night.*

"I want to see where Bruce Willis lives." Robinson looked up at me from underneath his bangs, his expression only slightly sheepish.

I felt like knocking my head against the table. Why did I keep expecting some profound declaration from him? Sometimes he made me wonder if the human adolescent male was a completely different species from the human adolescent female. (Different as in significantly less evolved.)

But this was his trip as much as mine, and I wanted to be a good sport. So after breakfast, we flagged down the nearest open-top tour van. The guide promised it would give us an *incredible* look at the stars' *jaw-dropping* homes, and a *secret window* onto their *enviable* lives.

I thought it might make me feel like a Peeping Tom, but Robinson had no such worries.

"If you don't want strangers staring at you, don't get famous," he said.

"I guess I should cancel my *American Idol* audition, then." I began to sing "I Will Always Love You"—a tough song for a good singer, and a devastating one for someone like me.

Robinson yelped and covered his ears.

Since we'd bought tickets for the Deluxe Route, we took our time on the tour, getting off one van, wandering around, and then hopping back on the next. We drove along the shopping districts of Melrose and Rodeo Drive; we passed beneath the towering palms of the Sunset Strip; we saw the La Brea Tar Pits and the Petersen Automotive Museum (which included a Hot Wheels Hall of Fame I never thought I'd pull Robinson away from).

It was late in the afternoon when we finally wound our way up into the hills.

"We're getting close, Axi," Robinson said, grinning. "Good ol' Bruce is going to invite us in to dinner."

"Sure," I said snidely. "Then we'll have dessert at Jennifer Aniston's house."

Robinson looked hurt. "Sarcasm doesn't become you, GG." But then his irrepressible smile shone again. "I bet Jen makes a wicked crème brûlée. She probably makes nice coffee, too, which is cool, because I like coffee with fancy desserts." He sounded utterly, completely sincere.

Crazy as it was, I loved this about Robinson: how he was capable of believing in something he didn't *actually* believe in. Does that make sense? He knew what he wanted to be true, what he felt should be true, and for a certain amount of time, by the power of his will (or his humor, or his stupid, boyish hope), it was true.

Believing in believing. Robinson was exceptional at that.

"On the left you will see the house formerly owned by Arnold Schwarzenegger," the tour guide called, interrupting my thoughts about Robinson and, no doubt, Robinson's thoughts about dessert.

Robinson leaned in close to me and whispered Arnold's most famous line: "'I'll be back.'"

"'Come with me if you want to live,'" I hissed—an Arnold quote from *Terminator 2*.

"Wait, I've got one—" He slapped his forehead, unable to recall it.

"'Hasta la vista, baby'?" I asked, smiling smugly.

"Gaah, it was on the tip of my tongue!" Robinson reached out and tickled me in the ribs, which made me squeal.

The tour guide kept talking, but we'd stopped listening. We drove through lush green neighborhoods, peering past iron gates and elaborate landscaping to catch glimpses of enormous mansions. The air smelled like roses...and money.

The driver slowed down around a particularly steep curve and then stopped to let a group of cyclists pass.

I grabbed Robinson's hand. "Let's split."

He turned to me, uncomprehending.

"Over the side," I whispered. And because he still didn't seem to get it, I showed him. I swung a leg over the edge of the open-top van and dropped down to the street.

If the other passengers noticed, they didn't say anything. A second later, Robinson landed beside me, looking utterly baffled. The van started up again and pulled away.

"So what's the brilliant plan now, Axi?" Robinson's hands were on his hips. "We don't know where Bruce Willis lives, and we're probably ten miles from our hotel."

I only smiled. "Follow me," I said. And I led him toward what I'd seen: a FOR SALE sign and a gate left open.

"Oh, duuuude," Robinson whispered, sounding suddenly like a K-Falls cretin. "Really?"

I looked up and down the street. Except for a lone gardener, whose back was to us, it was utterly deserted. We crept up the driveway, then alongside the vacant house to the back gardens. Whoever had lived in this ornate Mediterranean (estimated asking price: a cool five to ten mil) was gone, but the pool was still full, its water glassy and aquamarine blue.

The sun was on its way down and the sky was the color of persimmons. Robinson turned to me. "GG...," he began.

I threw my arms out and spun around. "If *this* hasn't proven to you I'm not a GG anymore," I asked, "what will?"

Robinson didn't say anything, but I already had an idea.

In one fluid motion, I stripped down to my underwear, tossed my clothes in a heap, and dove into the pool. I swam all the way to the bottom before rocketing back up in a cascade of glittering water droplets.

"Come in if you dare," I called to Robinson. *"Scalawag."*

He hesitated for a moment, but Robinson could never back down from a challenge. He took off his shirt, revealing his broad, pale chest, his flat stomach, and the low V of muscle there. I'd never seen that much of his skin before, and the ivory smoothness of it was startling.

Seeing him on the lip of the pool, naked now but for his boxers, I thought of Michelangelo's *David*. Not because Robinson had a perfect *David*-like body (though it was very nice) but because he had that combination of power and vulnerability that Michelangelo had given his sculpture. See, Michelangelo didn't show David triumphant, the way every other sculptor did. He showed David before he fought Goliath—when David believed he was doomed and went into battle anyway.

Robinson reached up to plug his nose, and he no longer looked remotely like a Renaissance hero. "Cannonball," he yelled on the way down. He came up spluttering. "Oh my God, it's cold!"

I laughed. "You mean invigorating," I said. "Revitalizing."

Robinson rolled his eyes at me. "Nerd. I can still call you *word nerd*, can't I?" Then he swam toward me, smiling, and he put his hands on my shoulders. Suddenly I was sure he was going to kiss me. He was so close, and his fingers were on my skin, and there was nothing—*nothing*—but water between us (and some flimsy, soaking-wet clothes).

He moved forward another step, and then he stopped. He opened his mouth like he was going to say something. But then he vanished under the water. The next thing I knew, he was

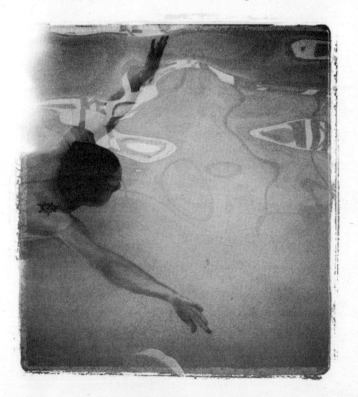

picking me up and tossing me backward into the deep end, and I was squealing, gasping, laughing, and he was saying, "Shhh, shhh, we don't want the cops to come."

We swam as evening fell and distant lights from the inhabited houses flickered on through the trees. I looked over at Robinson, who was floating on his back in the shallow end, and I wondered what it would be like to live in one of these castles.

I'd have everything money could buy, but it wouldn't be the same as having everything I wanted. Not even close.

14

WE WERE LUCKY THAT NIGHT. NOT ONLY
did we get away with trespassing, we got a ride home. The
gardener from across the street had seen us emerge, wet and
shivering, from the gate, and offered to drive us back to town.

"*Estás invadiendo*," he said, smiling. "*¿Sí?*"

Robinson nodded. "*Sí*," he said. "*Somos traviesos.*" He turned
to me. "That means 'we're naughty.'"

I was pressed up against his side in the front seat of the
truck, trying to find the warmth of him through our damp
layers of clothes. "See? You totally can't call me GG anymore,"
I said sleepily.

"Maybe BG," he suggested. "For Bad Girl."

My eyelids were so heavy, and then they were closing. "Or
MB. Mixed Bag…," I murmured.

And honestly, that was the last thing I remember. I must

have fallen asleep in the truck, and Robinson must have carried me up to the room and laid me down on our shared bed. Maybe he fluffed up the pillows for me, and maybe he even kissed me. But if he did, I'll never know.

I woke several hours later to find him staring at me.

"Before we leave, we should actually see a *star*," he said. "Not just a pink symbol on a sidewalk, or the house where one lives."

I burrowed under the covers. "Why can't we just turn on the TV? There're plenty of them there."

"We need to see one in real life," he insisted.

But this isn't real life, the old Axi Moore insisted. *This is a crazy adventure. And as great as it is, it can't last.*

Of course, as both the old and the new Axi well knew, real life didn't necessarily last, either.

I peeked my head out from the blankets, then ducked it back under again. Robinson was at the end of the bed, and he suddenly yanked the covers off me. I tried to grab them, but he was too strong. "Did you bring a nice dress?" he asked, raising one dark eyebrow at me.

I scoffed. "Runaways tend not to pack formal wear."

"Well, put on whatever you've got, because we're hitting the red carpet."

I assumed Robinson was pulling my leg, but I rose and took a quick shower, then put on the Forever 21 dress I'd packed just in case. I put on a little mascara, too, and a dab of lipstick.

His eyes lit up when he saw me emerge from the bathroom. "You clean up good, Axi Moore," he said. Robinson did, too. In a slightly rumpled oxford and a clean pair of jeans, he looked like an ad for Levi's 501s.

He led me down the hall and out to the street, where we hopped into a cab. "Now it's my turn to surprise you," he said. And then he held his hand over my eyes until we pulled up in front of the Hammer Museum. "Ta-da!" he said.

Ahead of us snaked a long line of black limos. There was red carpet laid over the sidewalk, and a bunch of people milling around, and a giant banner that said CHILDREN'S HOSPITAL LOS ANGELES ANNIVERSARY GALA.

I saw the word *hospital* and my stomach suddenly felt like it was full of stones. "What is this?" I asked.

"A benefit," Robinson said brightly. "A party. Major star power, because as you can imagine, no one in Hollywood wants to be accused of not helping sick kids." He climbed out of the cab and held out his hand. "Come on, let's go inside."

"*You* are a sick kid, Robinson," I said. "Mentally, I mean. They don't just let randoms crash the red carpet."

"But we're not randoms, as you so ungenerously characterize us. We are Axi and Robinson, the G-rated Bonnie and Clyde." He lifted me into the sunshine and smiled his dazzling smile. "If we don't belong here, who does?"

What could I do but laugh? "I think stealing a Harley ought to at least earn us a PG," I said.

"I'm in complete agreement," Robinson said. Then he held up a finger, signaling me to wait. "As the kids say, BRB."

He walked up to the nearest gatekeeper, a middle-aged woman dressed all in black. I watched as men in suits and women in jewel-colored cocktail dresses filed past her through the doors. The gatekeeper was trying to ignore Robinson, but I knew she wouldn't last. When Robinson turned on the charm ray, few could withstand it.

Sure enough, a moment later, she nodded and beckoned me over. As I approached, she looked at me with…concern, or maybe even pity. I shivered under her gaze. What exactly had Robinson told her? "You two go in over there," she whispered, and pointed toward a side entrance.

And then we were inside, and there were famous people *everywhere*. I saw Matt Damon talking to Mark Wahlberg by a potted fern, and Tina Fey posing in front of a giant stand of paparazzi. Camera flashes popped like fireworks, and in a matter of seconds, I was no longer worrying about what Robinson had said to the gatekeeper. All around us were bona fide superstars, talking and laughing and guzzling free drinks, just like regular people.

"I'm seeing a lot of excellent facial work," Robinson noted. Somehow he'd gotten his hands on a flute of champagne.

"'I love Los Angeles. I love Hollywood. They're beautiful. Everybody's plastic, but I love plastic,'" I said.

"Huh?"

"Andy Warhol said that."

Robinson held out his arm, and I tucked my hand in the crook of it, as if we were on our way to prom. He leaned in close, and I could feel his breath in my hair. "I told you we'd get in, didn't I?"

"And you were right," I said.

"Which makes you…?" He waited, an expectant smile teasing the corner of his mouth.

I sighed. "Wrong."

He laughed and pulled me close. "Axi admits fallibility," he said. "I'm going to treasure this moment forever."

My cheek pressed against his shirt, I smiled up at him. I would, too, I thought, but for a wholly different reason. Just days earlier we were in Klamath Falls, and now we were on the red carpet. What couldn't we do, as long as we were together?

15

THERE IS A LIMIT TO THE SUCCESS OF ANY partnership—and we discovered ours later that evening, when Robinson decided it was time to teach me to drive.

I said, "Robinson, I can't learn how to drive in a stolen car."

He shrugged. "It's just like any other car. Gas pedal on the right, brake on the left. Four gears forward, one reverse."

He was always so confident. But maybe that was because everything came easily to him: he could hot-wire a Harley, sweet-talk just about anyone, and play whatever musical instrument he was given. His free-throw percentage was ridiculous, and no matter where he was, he could always find true north.

Me, I was not so sure of myself. About anything. "I don't know how I feel about this," I said softly.

Robinson reclined the passenger seat and pretended to close

his eyes. "I feel good enough for both of us. Time for me to relax and enjoy riding shotgun."

I clenched my hands on the steering wheel. *You can do this, Axi*, I told myself. *You've played Grand Prix Legends!* Then came the other voice: *Yeah, and you sucked at it. You always crashed right out of the starting gate.*

"Ready?" Robinson asked.

I nodded, even though I wasn't. Robinson had to lean over and start the car, because I didn't know how to work the screwdriver.

"Okay. So check your mirrors and see if it's clear. Then you're going to step on the brake and shift into drive." He made it sound so easy, like I wasn't behind the wheel of a two-ton death machine.

I must have said this out loud, because Robinson said, "That is a *slight* exaggeration. We're in an empty parking lot, Axi. How much damage can you do?"

"I don't know," I said grimly. "We'll see."

For a second I thought of my physics class, the one I'd skipped the day I met Robinson at Ernie's dusty old counter. *A body at rest will remain at rest unless an outside force acts on it.* That's Newton's First Law. In other words, I was totally safe—until I stepped on the gas.

But I took a deep breath and somehow successfully shifted gears. When the car didn't explode, I forced myself to lightly press the gas pedal. The car moved forward. Slowly. Jerkily. But it moved. "Oh my God, I'm driving," I said.

Robinson grinned. "And the prize for stating the obvious goes to…Alexandra Moore!"

"Shut up," I squealed.

Robinson laughed. "Sorry—I couldn't resist. You're normally a much more subtle thinker."

"I hate you," I said, but I was laughing, too.

I was going twenty miles an hour and it felt like flying. I was also quickly nearing the edge of the parking lot. "What do I do now?"

"Why don't you try turning," Robinson suggested. "So we don't, I don't know, go barreling into traffic?"

I slammed my foot on the brake and whirled to face to him. Sure, I'd had a good thirty seconds of decent driving, but some things just weren't funny yet. "This is hard for me, you know!" I yelled.

Robinson reached over and put his hand on my arm. It was…calming. "Axi," he said gently, "is it really hard for you? Think about it before you answer."

I frowned. It was scary, yes. Unfamiliar. But hard? Well, not really. It was like Robinson said: gas pedal on the right, brake on the left. Four gears forward, one reverse.

All I needed to do was move forward.

It was almost as if Robinson could see the fear leaving my body. He gave my arm a squeeze. "See?" he said. "You get it. You're going to be fine."

And I was fine. I drove around the parking lot for almost an hour while Robinson, the human karaoke machine, sang driving songs: "On the Road Again," "I Get Around," and "Mustang Sally." I practiced turning, accelerating, and even parallel parking.

Finally Robinson said, "I think you're ready for the street."

I said, "I think I'm ready for you to stop singing."

"Deal."

So at the edge of the lot, I looked both ways—and then I pulled into traffic.

"Pedal to the metal, Axi!" Robinson said.

I was giddy, thrilled, scared. I was behind the wheel of a car, in fantastic Los Angeles, with the boy who was possibly the love of my life sitting next to me.

94

"Whoa, you cut that guy off there," Robinson said.

"I did?"

"Don't drive like you own the road; drive like you own the car."

"That's funny," I said, checking my mirrors and accelerating, "because I don't own it, and neither do you."

"*If I can just get off of this LA freeway / Without getting killed or caught,*" Robinson sang—it was some old country song.

Wasn't he supposed to not sing? "It's not a freeway," I pointed out.

And it was a good thing it wasn't, because what happened next would have been a lot worse.

The other part of Newton's First Law? *A body in motion will remain in motion, unless acted upon by an outside force.*

In this case, the outside force was a parking meter.

I don't know how it happened. One minute everything was fine, and the next minute we were at a dead stop and blood was pouring out of my nose.

16

DIZZY AND OVERWHELMED, I STARED out the window with a T-shirt held to my face as Robinson hurried us onto the 10. He'd handed me the shirt as he slid into the driver's seat. We had to leave the scene quickly—there were witnesses.

"You're okay, right?" he asked.

"I think so." My voice came out very small. I wasn't worried about my nose—I was worried about having smashed up a stolen car.

"Don't worry," Robinson assured me. "The LAPD's got way bigger fish to fry."

But his voice sounded sort of shaky. As if maybe he didn't have any idea what he was talking about. And he kept glancing in the rearview mirror, like he was watching for flashing lights.

"I'm sorry," I whispered. But I don't think he heard me.

His eyes darted from road to mirror and back again. "Well, Axi, in the immortal words of Dale Earnhardt Senior, 'You win some, you lose some, you wreck some,'" he said. "Every path has its puddle, you know? Nothing ventured, nothing gained! You can't make an omelet without breaking some eggs. And who wants to live in a world without omelets? Besides chickens, of course. I mean, I'm sure they'd be totally fine with it, ecstatic, really—"

"Robinson, you're babbling," I said.

"What?" He turned to me, his eyes flashing.

I took the shirt away from my face and felt a trickle of blood make its way down my lip. It tasted like salt. "You're babbling," I said. "Are you freaking out?"

His eyes widened. "Who, me? No! I'm not freaking out. Nope, no way! Not me."

"The fellow doth protest too much, methinks," I said, feeling suddenly woozier. Robinson was usually so calm; seeing him flustered definitely didn't make the situation better.

Robinson said, "Huh?"

"A slight modification of a *Hamlet* quote," I said weakly. I realized I was tapping my feet really quickly on the floor— almost like I was trying to run away inside the car.

"Are you speaking English?" he demanded. "Like, even now?"

I clenched my hands. It was my first real moment of doubt. Deep, profound doubt. As in, What were we *doing*? Was this whole trip the worst idea I'd ever had in my life?

I guess I must have said that out loud, too, because Robinson almost instantly calmed down. He took a long, deep breath, then leaned over and squeezed my knee. "We had a little adventure, and now it's time to be moving on," he said gently. "This trip is a brilliant idea, Axi. The best."

"Are you sure?" I asked. "Are we about to get caught?"

"No," Robinson said, this time sounding certain. "We're fine. Although we're missing a headlight and you have blood on your chin, which looks weird. Like maybe you're a vampire or something. But seriously. We're fine. We're better than fine. We're invincible. What's next on our itinerary?"

I couldn't believe how fast his mood had changed. But if Robinson felt confident again, I would try to, too. Because if I didn't trust him, what was I doing driving across the country with him?

"Well...Vegas, actually," I said. Yes, we were in over our heads—I understood that. But maybe things would still work out for us.

Robinson pounded the steering wheel. "Vegas, baby, here we come!"

I could hear the happiness in his voice. Part of me wanted to shake him, and the other part adored him for his unfailing optimism. How many times had I been in the pits of despair, only to have Robinson reach down a hand and haul me up into the sunlight? More than I cared to remember.

"It's all your fault, you know," I said, dabbing at my nose and chin.

He snorted. "I'm not the one who crashed."

"But you're the one who tried to teach me to drive."

"It's a life skill, Axi. I'm not going to be able to chauffeur you around forever." He turned to smile at me then. Maybe it was a trick of the light, but it seemed there was a new glimmer of melancholy behind his smile.

"Yes, you are," I said softly. But Robinson didn't reply.

17

WE DROVE ON THROUGH THE NIGHT.
The dark shapes of the Los Angeles hills gave way to flat
nothingness, and then, after a few hours, an orange glow blos-
somed in the sky. It grew steadily brighter, and when the
highway began its gentle slope downward, suddenly a vast
ocean of glittering lights stretched out below us.

"*Oooh, Las Vegas ain't no place for a poor boy like me,*"
Robinson sang. Then he turned to me. "That's Gram Parsons,"
he said. "Did you listen to that album I gave you?"

I hunched down in my seat, shaking my head minutely.

Robinson laughed. "Doesn't matter. I can sing the whole
damn thing for you."

"And you probably will," I said.

Humming, he drove us down the Strip, which was lit up
like Christmas times a million. It was as bright as day on the

street, even though it was after midnight. We passed signs for the Bellagio, Bally's, the MGM Grand—casinos I knew from *Ocean's Eleven* set in a landscape I knew from Hunter S. Thompson's *Fear and Loathing in Las Vegas*.

"So we have to gamble, right?" Robinson asked.

I nodded, suddenly resolute. "I believe it's required."

I cleaned myself up in a 7-Eleven bathroom while Robinson ate his ten thousandth Slim Jim. Then we went to the Luxor, mostly because it was shaped like a pyramid. It even had a giant Sphinx out front—an absurdity we just couldn't resist.

The moment we stepped inside, we were in yet another world. The sound of pinging slot machines, the smells of air-conditioning and sweat, the flashing lights above the pits: it was total sensory overload.

Robinson put his arm around my shoulders. "You want to win big?" he asked.

"Yeah, we've got twenty bucks to blow."

"Is that what your budget tells you? Well, that's two games of blackjack with a ten-dollar buy-in." He grinned. "That's assuming we don't win, which we will."

"Twenty dollars'll last longer at the slots," I said, because sitting in a semicircle with a bunch of strangers and trying to decide whether to tell the dealer to "hit me" was more than I was up for.

Robinson eyed the blackjack table longingly. He probably thought he could charm the cards into falling the way he wanted them to. Not me. Maybe I wasn't GG anymore, but I'd never be the gambling type. Because it was my babysitting money we were talking about, and I'd wrangled some serious brats to earn it.

Maybe it was just as well that a burly guy in a black vest came up to us as we headed for the slot machines. He wanted to see our IDs.

"Well, you see—" Robinson began.

The guy cut him off. "Save it. If you got an ID, you can play. If you don't, scram."

"Go on," I said to Robinson. "Now you can play a hand of cards. I'll wait outside."

He shook his head. "No way, Axi, we're in this together."

I liked the sound of that a lot. "Okay, what do you want to do now?"

Robinson yawned so deeply I decided not to wait for an answer. I said, "Let's go find a place to sleep."

So we pulled into the nearby parking lot of an Treasures, which at first I thought was a gift shop. "Why's it open so late? Who needs a snow globe at two A.M.?"

Robinson laughed—*at* me, not with me. "It's a strip club, you dope. This is Sin City, remember?"

I was too tired to take offense. I settled down in the back-seat and pulled my sweatshirt over me. Robinson snaked his hand around his seat in the front, and I reached out and took it. Here we were in the car again, three feet of air and eight inches of foam between us. *Why* hadn't I made a move at the hotel?

"Tell me a bedtime story," Robinson said.

"Sing me a bedtime song," I retorted.

"Flip a coin," he said.

I agreed, and he lost. So I fell asleep to Robinson singing, drumming lightly on the dashboard.

> *There was a girl named Axi*
> *who was a runaway.*
> *Instead of taking a taxi*
> *she tried to drive around LA.*
> *She crashed her car and hurt her nose*
> *and I don't mean to brag*
> *but who should rescue Axi*
> *but a charming scalawag?*

The sound of ringing laughter woke me at 4 A.M. A handful of dancers were leaving the club, done with their shift for the night.

One passed by the car and spied me in the backseat. "Hey, girl," she said, leaning in so close I could smell perfume and sweat. "You can't sleep here. They'll tow your car and take you and your friend here to the pound."

Robinson sat up, rubbing his eyes. "Huh?"

"Y'all need to be getting on home," said another. I could hear her smacking her gum. "Wherever that is."

Robinson leaned out the window and smiled at them like they were long-lost friends. "That is excellent advice," he said. "And I thank you for giving it. But unfortunately it is not possible for us to follow it at this time."

The women burst into laughter. One nudged the other with her bony hip. "Look at them! They're as cute as kittens. Chrissy, you take 'em home with you."

The blond one called Chrissy looked us over. She spent an especially long time looking at Robinson. "My car's the white Chevy over there," she said finally. "Y'all follow me out."

18

SUFFICE IT TO SAY THAT I DID NOT WANT
to go. What if Chrissy was an ax murderer?

But Robinson said that for one, the chances of that were
very slim; and for two, being killed with an ax was conceiv-
ably more appealing than spending another night with the
emergency brake poking into his side. So we followed Chrissy
toward the old Las Vegas Strip (the place they used to call
Glitter Gulch) and into a modest apartment complex.

"Here we go," she said, pointing toward a sagging red couch
in the middle of a dingy living room. Neon lights from the
signs outside reflected on the bare walls. "You sleep in there,
and your boyfriend can have the floor in the kids' room. It's
carpeted."

"He's not my boyfriend," I said, out of habit. I could see
Robinson getting ready to deliver his line—*She asked me out,*

but I turned her down—so I quickly added, "He's not my type."

Chrissy raised one thin, painted eyebrow. "Oh yeah? 'Cause looks to me like he'd be everyone's type."

Robinson, who seemed ready to fall over from exhaustion, made a show of kissing his biceps. He was such a beautiful goof—of *course* he was my type.

"Dork," I said.

"Nerd," he retorted.

Chrissy cackled. "God, you two are seriously the cutest things ever. If you aren't together, I don't know what your problem is."

Then she handed Robinson a pile of blankets and shoved him toward the door of a bedroom. "The kid on the left snores," she said. "Fair warning."

She gave me one last tired, vaguely maternal smile and disappeared into her bedroom. I lay on the soft couch and thought about what she'd said: that if Robinson and I weren't together, she didn't know what was wrong with us.

I didn't know, either. I mean, there was plenty wrong with us. But was that the thing keeping us apart?

I couldn't sleep, thinking about it. About him. Close to dawn, I tiptoed into the room where he was sleeping. He lay on his side, his hand tucked under his cheek. I watched him for a long time, counting his slow breaths and imagining I could hear the strong beat of his heart.

It sounded ridiculous even to me, but I couldn't stand not being near Robinson—especially now that I'd gotten to spend every night with him since we started this totally-insane-but-also-the-best-thing-ever trip. He made me feel the kind of joy I hadn't felt since I was a kid and my family was whole. And he also made me feel...a kind of rush I'd never felt before in my life.

How could I ever go back to being by myself—being without him—now that I knew these feelings were possible?

Before I knew what I was doing, I crept forward and lay down beside him, matching my breathing to his. Whether or not he wanted me the same way I wanted him, we were in this together—that was what Robinson had said. It had never occurred to me before what a complicated word *together* was.

19

I WOKE UP GASPING. THERE WAS A weight on my chest, crushing my heart, squeezing the air from my lungs. *So this is it*, I thought, *this is what it feels like to die.*

Next: *Oh my God, I haven't kissed Robinson yet. Except for that one time, ages ago, when I had that beer, which didn't even count...*

I clawed at the covers, my lungs screaming. My desperate fingers felt something hard and round—a small, bony knee.

There was a shriek, a high giggle, and suddenly the weight was gone. I sat up, dazed and blinking. There was a boy on the floor, gazing up at me with giant green eyes.

"My name is Mason Drew Boseman," he said pertly. "I'm four."

"You must weigh fifty pounds," I gasped, rubbing my sternum, where he'd just been sitting.

Then a small girl wandered in, clutching a dirty stuffed bunny. "That's Lila," Mason said. "She's two and she doesn't know how to use the potty."

"I'm...Bonnie," I said, my breath finally returning to normal. "Nice to meet you both."

Mason ducked his head, suddenly shy, like he hadn't just nearly killed me. Lila simply stared, then slowly brought her thumb up to her mouth and began to suck.

"Maybe I'll get up now," I said, untangling myself from the clean but ratty blanket. Still they stared.

I walked into the kitchen, following the smell of coffee. "Morning—" I began to say.

But I stopped. Because Chrissy, who was barefoot and in a silky red nightgown, had Robinson pressed up against the counter—and she was kissing him.

And it looked for all the world like he was kissing her back.

I turned around and stood shaking in the hall. Had I really just seen that? Was there a chance I was still dreaming? Mason looked up at me questioningly.

I counted to twenty, then coughed and tried to make it sound like I was coming down the hall to the kitchen. I heard the shuffling of feet, the screech of chair legs against linoleum.

This time when I rounded the corner, Robinson was at the kitchen table, reading the paper like he was the man of the house. "Morning, sunshine," he said, pushing a mug of steaming coffee toward me. He needed a shave, and there was a smudge of dirt on his cheek.

"He changed my oil, can you believe that?" Chrissy asked me. Her cheeks were flushed.

"That's not a metaphor for something, is it?" I asked, looking pointedly at Robinson.

He chose to ignore the question. "I woke up early. Thought I'd do a friend a favor."

That was Robinson. He never missed an opportunity to

help someone out. Apparently, he also never missed a chance to kiss someone—unless that person was me.

Chrissy had hopped up onto the counter, and she was looking at him like she was ready to ask him to move in. She might have two kids, but she was probably only a few years older than we were.

Mason tugged at my leg. "Did you know that dead squirrels can eat you? They have very sharp teeth. Dead squirrels are cool. Also dinosaurs are cool, and Batman, but Spider-Man is better because he got bitten by a spider." Mason began hopping up and down, narrowly missing my foot. "Superman can go into space because he can fly, but not Spider-Man because he needs a web and he can't shoot it in space because there's no buildings up there." His hopping had progressed to a wild bouncing.

Chrissy giggled. "I swear I don't give him coffee."

"He's charming," I said—through gritted teeth.

"I'm not charming. I'm starving!" Mason said.

I took a step forward. "Will you let me cook breakfast?" I asked. "So you can relax?"

Chrissy looked at me in surprise. "Uh…okay."

"You took us in—it's the least I can do." The fact was, I didn't know what to do with my hands, and cooking would calm me down. So I made omelets for everyone, with cheddar cheese and snippets of chives from a pot that Chrissy kept on her windowsill. I thought about undercooking her omelet and putting bits of eggshell in, but I reminded myself that she wasn't really the wrongdoer. I'd told her Robinson wasn't my boyfriend, so as far as she knew, he was available.

Not that I totally forgave her.

"Wow, I lucked out bringing you two home," Chrissy said, her mouth full of eggs. "This is the best omelet I've ever had."

"I've made a lot of them," I said. "I'm no gourmet or anything."

Robinson pointed his fork at me. "Not true. She can cook anything. She'll make someone a good little wife someday."

"Watch it," I warned.

"It's a compliment," Robinson insisted.

"I didn't take it as one," I said.

"You guys bicker like a brother and sister," Chrissy said, giggling. Then she looked serious again. "Do your parents know where you are?"

I turned back to the stove. "We plead the Fifth."

"We're on vacation," Robinson said.

Chrissy sighed and leaned back in her folding chair. "Okay," she said, "I won't pry. Everyone's entitled to their secrets. But here's a piece of advice: get out of Las Vegas, okay? Because you come here and you just get stuck."

She gazed toward the window then, the one that looked out over the Neon Boneyard, where old signs go to die.

Something told me that getting stuck was exactly what had happened to her.

I looked at Robinson, who was dumping sugar into his coffee. We'd never get stuck anywhere, not even if we wanted to. There was an undeniable reason for that—but it was one of our secrets.

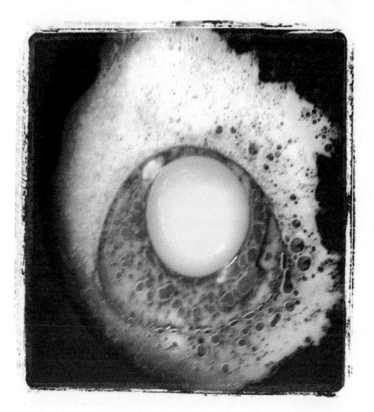

20

"I DON'T WANT TO TALK ABOUT IT."

So said Robinson when I asked him what he was doing tonsil-diving with a Las Vegas stripper at nine o'clock in the morning. (As if it would have been just fine later in the day.)

"Well, I want to talk about it," I said. I had dragged him and our few belongings outside as soon as breakfast was over, trying to avoid giving Chrissy a chance to ask us to stay.

Robinson looked at me for a moment, his expression unreadable, and then he turned and walked away. He wound through the cars parked near the Neon Museum, shaking his head and seemingly talking to himself.

I felt so helpless. Was I crazy? Had I imagined the romantic tension between us? What if Robinson had never wanted anything from me but my friendship? If that turned out to be true, then it was too bad Chrissy wasn't actually an ax murderer—because I was going to die a long, slow death of humiliation.

I wiped a bead of sweat from my lip. It was 10 A.M. and already hot. I sat down on the toe of a giant metal high-heeled shoe, which used to be part of the sign for the Silver Slipper Saloon.

I *hated* Las Vegas.

"What are you doing?" I finally called to Robinson.

He didn't answer—he was still pacing. I wasn't about to follow him up and down the street, so I stared at all the dead signs. There was one that said WEDDING CHAPEL and another right next to it that said SIN.

I thought about all the people who had come to Vegas looking for love or money, and what a minuscule percentage of them must have actually found it.

Robinson appeared at my side, and even though he was finally saying something, it wasn't anything I was interested in. I'd listen when he explained the kitchen kissing. In the meantime, I'd keep looking at the signs: GOLDEN NUGGET, JOE'S LONGHORN CASINO...

Then Robinson grabbed my arm and turned me toward him. He said, "The thing about a Boxster is, it eats tires. Especially if you dump your clutch. But since we aren't in this for long-term ownership..."

I scrutinized the shoe's peeling paint. "I don't know what you're talking about."

Robinson sighed, exasperated. "I'm talking about a Porsche,

Axi, because we're taking one." He pointed to a low black shape a hundred yards off. "It's an older model, so it won't have a tracking system. Hard to steal cars that send out little beacons to the LVPD, you know?"

Finally I looked at him. "We have a car already."

"I'm sick of it," Robinson said. "We need a better one." He kicked at the tip of the shoe.

"I don't want to steal another car," I said.

"Oh, my beloved Aximoron—*you* don't have to," he said. He flashed me his beautiful grin, then bounded away.

I clenched my fists and stared up at the white desert sky. Robinson was crazy—*He kisses some girl and then calls me his beloved? What gives?*

There was a screech of tires as Robinson pulled up in front of me. "Get in," he ordered.

If I didn't, would he drive off without me? Honestly, he looked like he might. It was times like these when Robinson seemed like the bad boy my father always claimed he was.

I barely had my seat belt on before Robinson gunned the engine and peeled out into the street. He was going sixty-five before I even blinked.

"That's what I meant by dumping the clutch," he said calmly. "In case you wondered."

I stared out the window, refusing to look at him. "I didn't," I said.

We were heading out of town, leaving the glittering lights and broken promises of Las Vegas behind us. Quickly.

"Slow down," I told him.

Robinson only laughed. "Speed never killed anyone! It's suddenly becoming stationary…that's what gets you."

I crossed my arms. "Yeah, if a thousand other things don't get you first," I huffed.

But it was Robinson's turn to ignore me. He began to whistle Bruce Springsteen's "Born to Run," and he kept on doing it, over and over, until I was ready to beg him to stop.

Then he saw the flashing lights coming up behind us, and suddenly I didn't have to.

21

*OBJECTS IN MIRROR ARE CLOSER THAN
they appear*. That's what your car's side mirror will tell you, but
I am here to say that the minute you can make out that the
object you see is a police car, it is already way too close.

"Robinson," I hissed, panic rising in my voice.

"Maybe they're not after us," he said. "I was only going...
hmm, twenty miles over the speed limit. Heck, it's practically a
crime to go any slower around here. This is Las Vegas, baby—
everything's legal but good behavior."

I could tell by the sound of his voice that Robinson didn't
believe this but wanted me to. He didn't want me to be afraid.
He never had, for as long as I'd known him.

"Pull over to the right-hand shoulder." The amplified,
crackling voice came through a megaphone mounted on the
side of the police car.

Robinson glanced down at the speedometer as if checking to see how high the numbers went. Like he was wondering if he should try to outrun the guy.

"Don't even think about it," I warned. "Do what the policeman says."

"You don't sound much like Bonnie," he said reproachfully.

"For God's sake, this isn't a movie. This is life! *Pull over!*"

I was reaching for the wheel to yank it to the right when Robinson slowed, flicked on his turn signal as polite as you please, and eased onto the right shoulder.

"See? I can follow directions," Robinson said. He tried to keep his tone light.

But it didn't matter now. I put my face in my hands. We were caught. I saw the headlines, the court-appointed lawyer, the hideous orange jumpsuit they'd make me wear. Was I old enough to be tried as an adult?

"It's going to be okay," Robinson said quietly.

Liar, I thought.

The officer approached Robinson's window. From my angle I could see only his belt and the soft, round stomach above it. "License and registration," he said gruffly.

Not even a "please."

"Sir," Robinson began, "is there a problem?"

The officer's hand shot out. "License and registration," he said again.

Robinson smiled ingratiatingly. "I believe I was going the speed of traffic—perhaps it was a trifle fast—"

"License and registration."

Robinson turned to me, his eyes wide. "He seems to have a somewhat limited vocabulary," he whispered, and to my horror, I almost burst into giddy laughter.

I covered my mouth as Robinson made a show of rooting around in the glove compartment. "It's in here somewhere," he said.

The cop began tapping impatiently on the roof of the car. Then he leaned in and looked at both of us carefully. He had small, mean eyes and an angry mouth. "Not many kids got a car this nice," he said. "You'd think their folks'd teach 'em how to drive it. But spoiled little rich kids—they don't listen to their parents much, do they?"

It was the first time in my life anyone had ever mistaken me for rich.

"I liked him better when he didn't talk," I whispered to Robinson.

Robinson pulled out the registration and handed it over. The cop inspected it. "License," he said.

"Sir, this is all a mistake," Robinson said. "I'm very sorry for speeding. If you'll just let us go with a warning, I promise I'll never do it again."

The cop barked out a laugh. "I heard that one before. There's a sucker born every minute, son, but you're not looking at one." He stared philosophically down the highway and then turned back to us. "See, these rich kids," he went on, his eyes narrow and cold, "if their folks can't teach 'em things, the law has to. The law just loves to give lessons."

Robinson was so used to charming people. I'd seen him talk his way out of detentions, and into a Hollywood party, and everything in between. So now he looked as though he couldn't believe what he was hearing. But he nodded. "Of course, sir. I understand. I'm going to have to get out, though. I keep my wallet under my seat, and I can't reach it from in here. May I step out, sir?"

The cop backed away. Robinson reached over and grabbed my hand. Hard. "Bonnie," he whispered.

"What?" I asked. But he was already out of the car, and I could still feel the pressure of his fingers on my skin.

I saw it all through the window. At first Robinson kept his hands in the air, to show the cop he meant no harm. But the next thing I knew, there was a flash of movement, a grunt, and then a holler of rage.

Robinson yelled, "Get out, Bonnie, I need you!"

Without thinking, I obeyed. And that was when I saw the love of my life—car thief, trespasser, and kisser of strippers—pointing a gun in a young cop's face.

I nearly fell to my knees. I reached out to the hood of the Porsche to steady myself. The metal of the gun glinted in the desert sunlight. *This can't be happening*, I thought. *This is definitely a dream or a scene from a movie—or a hallucination or something.*

Robinson half-turned to look at me and, I swear to God, *winked.*

My jaw dropped. If I'd thought he was a little crazy before, now I was sure he'd gone utterly insane. Then I saw that tiny smile flicker at the corner of his mouth. That smile I knew better than my own. It said to me: *This is all a game, Axi. No one's going to get hurt.*

I took a step toward them, and I prayed that he was right.

"I'm really sorry that I have to do this," Robinson said, turning back to the cop, "but you gave me no choice."

The cop's face was red and glistening. He was silent, full of brutal but impotent rage. He seemed to have lost the power of speech altogether.

I looked up and down the road, watching for traffic. Never had I been gladder that Robinson stuck to the back routes.

"Bonnie," Robinson said, "you take his cuffs and put them on him."

Fumblingly, I did as I was told. When I snapped the metal around his wrist, the cop flinched. "I'm so sorry," I blurted. "Are they too tight? I don't want them to be too tight, but I don't exactly know how to work them."

The cop merely turned redder in the face.

Robinson was jittery, like he might jump out of his flannel. Even on a back road, someone could drive by at any

moment. "Again, I'm really sorry about this, sir. It's just that we're on a mission. We have to keep moving. It's a life-or-death situation."

The red-faced cop cleared his throat like he was going to say something. But then his mouth contorted and opened, and he spit. A whitish glob of mucus landed right on the tip of Robinson's cowboy boot.

"Well, that was rude," Robinson said, sounding shocked.

As if the cop should be more polite. I wondered if Robinson

had somehow hit his head in our fender bender and the blow had knocked his conscience out of whack.

"You kids have no idea the trouble you're going to be in," the cop suddenly bellowed. His anger and his scarlet face frightened me. I could hardly look at him.

Maybe it wasn't the cop who was the problem—maybe it was us. The teen outlaws.

Maybe I was kind of terrified of who we'd so quickly become. We'd just threatened a police officer with his own gun and locked him up with his own handcuffs!

How had our trip gotten so out of control after I had mapped it out to perfection?

And why...didn't I care anymore?

I suddenly felt exhilarated. Unstoppable. This was the moment to make a real choice about the rest of my life, no matter how afraid I was to do it.

I steeled myself and dragged my eyes up to meet the cop's. "We're not going to get caught," I said.

I said it softly but firmly. It was a promise. A prayer. A wish.

22

Robinson took a step back from the cop, using the gun to point toward the door of the police car. "Bonnie," he said to me, "you're going to need to drive the cruiser." He turned to the cop. "I haven't taught her how to drive a stick yet," he explained.

By now I was nearly numb with shock, but I climbed into the driver's seat of the black-and-white. Gas pedal, turn signal, ignition. Everything looked to be in pretty much the same place. Meanwhile Robinson was gently shoving the cop into the back. Thank goodness for the glass between us, because, even cuffed, that guy petrified me. If looks could kill, Robinson and I would have been goners.

"You gonna be all right?" Robinson asked me, poking his head in the front window.

I put both hands on the wheel, one at ten and one at two.

I tried to seem like I wasn't having a small heart attack. "Well, there aren't any parking meters to hit."

He gave me a crooked smile. Maybe it was totally inappropriate, but I needed it.

"Awesome, you're good to go, then. Now follow me," he said. He got into the Porsche, drove a little way, then took a dirt road off to the left. We followed it for a couple of miles, passing nothing but dirt and scrubby sage.

I refused to look into the rearview mirror because I could practically feel the death glare the police officer was giving me. I was so on edge from the last fifteen minutes that I knew if I met his eyes I was going to freak out completely, crash, and end up killing us both. I was gripping the steering wheel so tightly that my fingers were turning white.

When Robinson stopped, I braked too hard and scrambled out of the car, barely remembering to put it in park.

"Whoa," Robinson said, catching me by the elbow as I stumbled toward him. "Everything okay? He's all locked up in back?"

"No, I let him out," I snapped, yanking my arm away. *Breathe*, Axi. "Sorry. Nerves."

"Let's get out of here."

"But—" I glanced back at the police car. The cop was sitting motionless in the back, but I thought I could hear him cursing.

"Someone will find him, don't worry," Robinson said, pointing into the distance at what looked like tract houses—or a mirage. Everything was flat all around us. The desert was so empty. There wasn't even a cactus.

DID YOU...
LOCK YOUR CAR?
CLOSE THE WINDOWS?
POCKET THE KEYS?
DO NOT LEAVE VALUABLE
IN PLAIN SIGHT.
BE AWARE OF YOUR
SURROUNDINGS.

Robinson took my arm again and led me toward the Porsche. When we were strapped in, he gunned the engine, and we shot out of there in a great cloud of dust that billowed up so high it hid our crime completely.

"We've got to ditch the Porsche," Robinson said as he pulled onto the main road. For some reason he was heading back into town.

Suddenly I began to shake. My legs jumped and twitched and even my teeth were chattering. Had we just done what I thought we did? "Robinson—" I said.

"What?" He looked at me, concerned.

"I can't steal a car right now. My nerves can't take it."

"No problem," Robinson answered. "We can go back to Axi's Plan A."

"I don't even remember what that *is*," I moaned.

"The bus, of course—petri dish for superbacteria. Because I don't know about you, darlin', but I'm just itching for some kind of dreadful infection." Then Robinson grinned maniacally.

"Tell me—honestly. Have you lost. Your. Mind?"

As usual, Robinson ignored my question and instead pulled into a bus station on the edge of the city. "There it is! Our ticket to bacterial meningitis."

We got our backpacks and left the Porsche in a fire lane. I just wanted to be gone. I didn't have time to write a thank-you note to the owner, but it was probably just as well. Now that we were bona fide criminals, we should try to leave fewer clues behind.

Inside the station, it was dark and cool and grimy. All my adrenaline-fueled courage had faded, and I wanted to curl up in a ball in the corner. "Where do we go? We were supposed to see the Great Sand Dunes next," I whispered.

Robinson scanned the departure board. "Interesting," he said. "Because these famous dunes of sand happen to be near Alamosa, Colorado, correct?"

I frowned in confusion. "How did you know that?"

"My dear, that bus leaves in moments. See?" Robinson pointed. "The luck of the traveler is with us." He was already walking toward the ticket booth, one hand reaching for his wallet.

Could it really be that simple? "I thought it was luck of the Irish," I called weakly.

He turned around and shrugged. "Who cares? We've got

our ride. But for your information, my grandma was an Irish rose from County Cork."

I looked at him in surprise, because Robinson never, ever talked about his family. "Okay, but what about the cop?" I asked, hurrying up to him. "We can't just leave him. We have to call someone."

"I thought you weren't GG anymore," Robinson said.

I couldn't tell if he was joking or not. "Just because I want to make sure someone doesn't die of heatstroke?" I found an old pay phone and fished in my pockets for change. I told the woman who answered that I'd been out riding my horse when I'd come upon a cop car in the middle of nowhere. I made myself sound young and stupid, but I gave all the necessary details.

She wanted to know my name. "Carole Ann," I said.

"You did a good thing, Carole Ann," she said.

Lady, if only you knew.

23

THERE'S AN OLD SAYING ABOUT HOW ONLY
the guilty sleep well in jail. The innocent man stays awake all
night, freaking out, while the guilty one sleeps like a baby. He
figures he's finally where he belongs and he might as well get
some shut-eye.

Robinson and I weren't in jail, of course—we were on a
Greyhound. But it was uncomfortable and smelly and con-
fined, the way I imagined jail to be. And we hadn't been on
the bus more than five minutes before Robinson leaned over,
put his head on my lap, and fell asleep.

Guilty, I thought. *We're both so guilty.*

For a while I stared out the window, watching the flat,
dry land go by. I still couldn't believe the way things had
turned. A few hours ago, Robinson making out with someone else was just about the worst of my problems. Now? Try

felony assault, grand theft auto, and who knew what else.

Back in the moment, of course, what we'd done made perfect sense. We'd *had* to do it. A stolen Porsche, a hijacked gun, and suddenly cuffing and abandoning a cop seemed like a fine idea because, hey, it would keep us out of juvie.

For now, I thought darkly.

Reality came down on me with a crushing weight. What in the world had we done? This was supposed to be a road trip—a lark—and it was turning into a crime spree. What would we do next? Steal a kid's lunch money? Rob a bank?

In the seat ahead of us an old lady was knitting. I could

hear her needles sliding and clicking. Every once in a while she'd turn around and smile at me. At first I smiled back, but then I started to get nervous. Was it possible she knew something? Could she read the guilt on my face? Did the Nevada police employ undercover agents old enough to collect Social Security?

I shook Robinson awake. He sat up, rubbing his eyes, and gave me a grumpy look.

"We can never do anything like that again," I said quietly. "Ever."

Robinson ran his hand through his tousled hair and sighed. "I know, Axi. Do you think I wanted it to happen like that? You know that's not me. But we couldn't let him stop us." His dark eyes, with their heavy lashes, searched my face. He wanted to be sure I knew he'd done the only thing he could. "I don't want this to end," he said. "Not yet. Do you?"

I shook my head. I wanted to go on like this with him forever, except I wanted more kissing and less crime. "What if we'd—" I began, but Robinson held up a hand.

"There's no point in what-ifs. What's done is done."

"You sound like my mother," I said. "Who, I have lately realized, was usually full of BS."

Robinson grinned, then faced forward and said hi to the old lady, who'd turned to look at us again. "It was total insanity, I admit that," he whispered to me when she turned back around. "But it's over, okay, Axi? Everything is going to be fine. In the words of Irving Berlin, one of the greatest songwriters ever, from here on out, there's nothing but blue skies."

Maybe I'm an idiot—actually, I'm definitely an idiot—but hearing him say that made me feel better.

Robinson reached out and brushed a piece of hair from my cheek. "I never want anything bad to happen to you, Axi," he said quietly. "And while I have not yet been in one, I suspect that jail is bad."

"You think it's worse than a pediatric cancer ward?" I blurted.

Robinson seemed to pale. Then he laid his head on my lap again. "I promise," he said, "we'll never do something like that again."

"Pinkie swear," I said, holding out my little finger.

We shook on it.

"And Axi?" He looked up at me from below, his eyes wide and deep enough to drown in.

"What?"

"I'm sorry about Chrissy. Honestly, she came on to me. It took me by surprise. And I didn't want to be rude."

I sighed. Robinson was the only guy in the world who could deliver that line and actually have me believe it. "Yeah, I know how much you dislike rudeness," I said.

"I do," Robinson said, closing his eyes. His voice grew sleepy again. "Rudeness is so…rude…"

I smiled. And then I rested my head against the greasy bus window and fell asleep.

24

WE GOT OFF AT THE ALAMOSA STOP AND stuck out our thumbs, trying to look wholesome and innocent. When that didn't work, Robinson told me it was time for me to show some leg.

"*You* show it," I countered. "You're the one who always charms everyone." (Also? I hadn't shaved since we left home.)

"Except that cop," he said ruefully.

Eventually, a nice old man in an El Camino pulled up. We told him we were headed to the Great Sand Dunes National Park, and he nodded approvingly and drove us right up to the visitors' center. He wouldn't even take ten bucks for gas.

Instead, he slipped me a twenty as I was pulling my backpack from underneath the seat. "Go out for dinner tonight," he urged. "Y'all need some meat on your bones." For a moment he gazed wistfully at the sand dunes, gleaming golden at the base of blue, snow-capped mountains. "If my Meg was alive, I'd call her up and tell her to put a roast in the oven." His eyes seemed to film over. Then he snapped back to the present. "Take care of yourselves, all right?" And then he drove away.

I tried to shake off the strange, sad feeling his good-bye had given me. I looked over at Robinson, who was waving at me from the edge of a creek that cut along the base of the dunes.

"It's like someone picked up a piece of the Sahara and put it down in Colorado," he said when I approached.

"It's amazing," I said, snapping a picture that I knew wouldn't do it justice. "Why do people end up in towns like K-Falls when there are places like this in the world?"

"That's an excellent question," Robinson said. He flung his arms out wide, as if he could hug the whole huge vista. "We should probably never go back." He looked pretty pleased by that idea.

We began walking up a ridge to the top of the dunes. It was tough going—the sand was loose, and our feet sank deep into it. I could hear Robinson breathing hard behind me. As we neared the top, the wind picked up the sand and flung it, stinging, against us.

"It's like full-body exfoliation," Robinson said, wiping the grit from his face. "There are people who pay good money for this."

"The glass is always half-full for you, isn't it?" I asked. I would have smiled, but I'd have gotten sand in my teeth. Optimism was one of his best qualities.

Stinging sand aside, we arrived in a spot that was breath-
taingly beautiful. On nearby dunes we saw some people hiking
up and others sliding back down on what looked like snow-
boards. Their delighted shouts carried through the air, which
was already shimmering with heat.

Robinson began to strum an imaginary guitar: *"Even castles
made of sand..."* Then he looked at me somewhat sheepishly.
"Jimi Hendrix."

"I know," I told him. "My dad has that album." I squinted
into the distance. Beyond the dunes, the prairie was full of
yellow wildflowers. I held my camera at arm's length and took
a picture of us squinting and grinning, on top of the world.

We might have hiked back down then, but I turned and saw an old plastic sled half-buried in the sand. I pointed, and Robinson's eyes lit up. "Are you thinking what I'm thinking?" I asked, but I knew he was, so I didn't wait for an answer.

I climbed onto the front of the sled, and Robinson stood behind me, his hands on my back. He began to run, pushing me, and then he leapt in. He wrapped his arms around my waist and buried his head in my hair as we raced down the slope. The wind whipped the sand into my face but I didn't care—I screamed with delight.

At the bottom of the dune, we lay on the sand, breathless.

"Wow," Robinson said.

"Who needs snow?" I yelled, flinging up my arms. "Want to go again?"

Of course he did.

We spent a giddy, thrilling hour hiking up and then racing down, after which we were so hot and tired we could barely move.

"I'm dying of thirst," Robinson said, collapsing at my feet. "Also I think my nose is fried."

"'What makes the desert beautiful is that somewhere it hides a well,'" I said.

"Huh?" Robinson asked, rubbing his nose.

"It's a line from *The Little Prince*."

"You and your books," he said teasingly.

"It wouldn't kill you to read one."

He raised a dark eyebrow. "You never know. It might," he said, and smiled. "So where's that well, then?"

I tossed him a water bottle from my backpack, but it arced wide. He scrambled to get it, then opened the lid and drained the liquid in about two seconds.

"You're lucky I've got another one for myself," I chided. "Otherwise that would've been very greedy. Very scalawag-ish."

He snorted. "I know you, Axi. Of course you have extra water. Now I'm going to close my eyes. Wake me in ten." Then he fell asleep, just like that, at the bottom of a sand dune.

We washed off the grit in cold, clear Medano Creek, and we set up our tent at a nearby campground. After dinner—canned chili heated over the fire—we stored our food and packs in the metal bearproof box on the edge of the campsite.

Night came suddenly, as if someone had blown out the sun like a candle. And then the stars burst from the sky, more than I'd ever seen in my life. I stared up, dazzled, and by this point almost too spent to speak.

Robinson looked up, too. "There's something I wanted to say to you that I never got a chance to," he said.

I knew not to get my hopes up by now. "What's that?" I asked.

"You throw like a girl."

"You are such a jerk," I said, laughing. I picked up the rinsed-out chili can and took aim. "I'll show you throwing like a girl!"

"I'm kidding. Those are the last lines from the movie *Sahara*," he said. "Since we spent the day in the desert and all."

I put the can back down. I was too exhausted to throw, anyway. Instead, I took a deep drink of water. And I looked at the long, lean shape of Robinson through the darkness, thinking that there were many different kinds of thirst.

25

WE STOLE A PICKUP JUST AFTER DAWN, as the sun was rising golden over the mountains.

Isn't it crazy, how matter-of-factly I can say that?

Well, Your Honor, we ate breakfast, and then we stole a truck. Granola bars and a Chevy, sir, if specifics matter to the court.

If I ever meet that judge, I'm sure he'll ask me, "Did you two think you were invincible?" And I'll look him right in the eyes. "No, sir," I'll tell him. "In fact, I thought the opposite."

The engine of our borrowed truck was loud and rattling, and the radio played only AM stations. "This thing needs a new muffler," Robinson said, frowning. "The exhaust manifold could be cracked, too."

"Awesome, a broken getaway car," I said. "And wow, are

we listening to *Elvis* right now?"

"*Love me tender, love me true,*" Robinson sang. Then he stopped abruptly. "It's not like I had time to give it a checkup before I stole it." Was it just me, or did that sound a little…huffy? "Anyway, variety is the spice of life, and we can trade up at the next stop. Would you care to tell the chauffeur where that is, Ms. Moore?"

I shrugged. The next stop I'd planned was Detroit, fourteen hundred miles away. "I don't know. The world's biggest ball of stamps? Carhenge? The Hobo Museum?" We were driving northeast, toward Nebraska, heading into what residents of

the East and West Coasts liked to call flyover country.

"Carhenge?" Robinson asked, sounding interested. "I bet that's like Stonehenge, but with cars."

"Wow, ten thousand points for you," I said. He gave me a hurt look. "I'm sorry," I mumbled.

I was irritable because I'd been awake most of the night. And it wasn't the claustrophobic tent or the hard ground; it was Robinson. What was I supposed to do about him? About us? We'd been through so much together—and our journey had started well before the trip began. Wasn't it time for me to tell him how I felt (even if I wasn't exactly sure how to describe it)?

I spent a long time thinking about what I'd say, and revising my lines, but in the end I was about as successful as I'd been with my good-bye note to Dad. As in: Not. At. All.

Sample: *Robinson, I think I loved you from the first moment I saw you.* (But I was high on painkillers that day, so I loved everyone.) *When I look at you, I see a better version of myself.* (Wait—so I want to kiss myself?) *I don't know what I'd do without you in my life.* (Um…not steal cars?)

It was stupidly, infuriatingly impossible. No wonder I hadn't written anything decent in ages—I couldn't even figure out how to tell a boy that I loved him. That whenever I looked into his eyes, I felt like I was drowning and being saved, all at the same time. That if I had to choose between dying tomorrow or spending the rest of my life without him, I would seriously consider picking imminent death.

I was afraid of what I felt. But was that the only reason it was so hard to admit it to him? Or was I afraid that he didn't feel the same? Yes, I was definitely afraid of that.

Now, as we drove in silence through the wide-open morning, I wanted so much to slide over to his side of the bench seat. I wanted to put my hand on his leg and feel the answering tremor go through him. I wanted to say, *Pull over and kiss me.*

I took a deep breath. I couldn't sneak over toward him, inch by cowardly inch. I was just going to have to go for it. *All or nothing, Axi. Now is the time.*

I closed my eyes, offering a prayer to the gods of young love, Cupid or Aphrodite or Justin Bieber: *Don't let this be a terrible mistake.*

When I opened my eyes again, I saw that the truck was drifting to the right.

"Robinson?" I said, my voice rising as we veered toward the shoulder.

He didn't answer, and I looked over. His face was so pale it looked almost blue. He began to cough—a terrible, racking, wet sound that came from deep within him.

He looked at me and his eyes were full of fear.

And suddenly he was vomiting.

Blood.

"Stop the truck!" I screamed, reaching for the wheel.

We were already on the shoulder, and Robinson somehow managed to hit the brake while still gagging. Cars whizzed past us, shaking the cab with their speed.

"Oh my God, Robinson!" I cried, moving toward him. I was holding out my hands as if I could catch the blood—as if I could stop it from coming out of him and then put it back inside, where it belonged.

The air swam in front of my eyes. I was crying.

After a horrible, endless moment, Robinson stopped coughing. He wiped his red-streaked mouth with the sleeve of his flannel shirt.

"It's not that much, really," he said weakly, looking at his shirt. "I'm okay now."

But I knew this if I knew anything: *Robinson is not okay.*

Then again, it was possible that I wasn't, either.

part Two

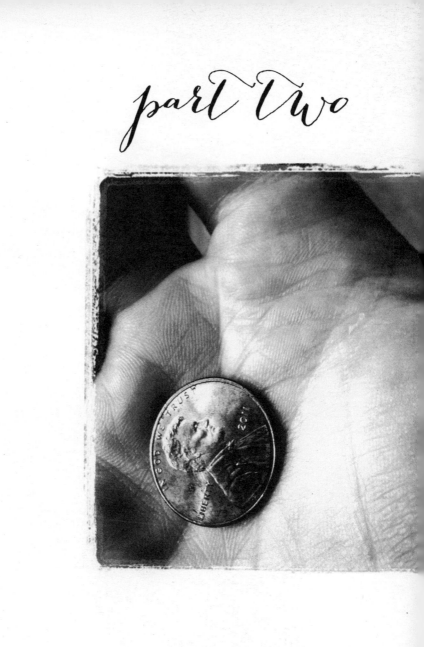

26

AND SO NOW, UNDER A COLORADO SKY
so blue it hurt my eyes, we arrived at the terrible truth. You
can plot your escape, you can ditch your life and your family,
and you can race down a two-lane highway in a stolen car. But
there are things you can never outrun.

Things like cancer. Because that comes along for the ride.

I managed to get us to a hospital forty-five minutes up the
road in La Junta. Robinson lay with his head in my lap, and I
ached to run my fingers through his hair and tell him everything would be all right. But because the truck didn't have
power steering, I needed both hands on the wheel.

And I wasn't sure that everything *would* be all right, not
at all.

The small hospital waiting room was freezing cold, lit with
the kind of harsh fluorescent light that makes people look as

gray as fish. Robinson shivered and leaned against me. There was a bloom of dark blood on his T-shirt. He buttoned his flannel self-consciously. "Otherwise I look like I've been stabbed," he explained.

"I'm not sure that's a bad thing," I said. There were four other people in the waiting room, and by the looks on their faces, they'd been there awhile.

Robinson shook his head. "I just need to sit down," he said in a raspy voice.

The woman at the desk glanced at me warily as I approached. Maybe she saw the fear in my eyes—or maybe she thought I was homeless or on drugs. I could see my pale reflection in the corner of a mirror, and I couldn't exactly blame her.

"Can I help you?" she asked. Her name tag read DEBBIE.

"My friend is sick," I said, pointing to Robinson, who was huddled on a plastic chair in the corner. The scene in the truck played over and over in my mind. It was nightmarish.

"The doctor has been paged," Debbie said. She inspected my face, frowning lightly. "Do you need to see him, too?"

"I'm absolutely fine," I said stiffly, even though I felt like I might collapse from exhaustion.

I rejoined Robinson, and we sat in the corner for what felt like hours. Eventually, an old man with his arm in a cast leaned over and put his good hand on my knee.

"It's a Saturday morning, hon," he offered. "Most of the doctors and whatnot are fishing."

I bit my lip, hard. We had no doctor. And when we got

one, I knew what it would mean: blood workups, fine-needle aspiration biopsies, positron-emission tomography scans....The thought of going through this again made me want to run and hide.

"Welcome to small-town America, Axi," Robinson said, "where the bowling alley and the Elks lodge have larger staffs than the hospital."

"Don't worry, the doctor is coming," I said. "Hey, in the meantime, we can watch TV. I know you haven't been getting your daily dose lately."

Robinson nodded. "If only you had a Slim Jim and a box of Oreos, everything would be perfect."

I tried to wipe a spot of blood from his collar. "You really have to eat better."

"I know," Robinson said. "I'm in the ER because of too many Slim Jims and not enough TV." He looked at me slyly.

Oh, if only that were true, I thought. For just a moment I clung to a wild hope that the doctor would give him a spoonful of extra-strength Maalox, and then we could be on our way to the Gateway Arch in St. Louis, or the world's largest ball of twine. But I'd seen his blood, the way it was dark, almost coffee-colored. I knew that meant it came from his gastrointestinal tract—where the cancer had been.

Where maybe it still was.

"Why do they have to pick the Home Shopping Network?" Robinson asked.

I looked up. A lady with long red nails was selling figurines, smiling at the camera with glossy lips and blindingly white teeth. "Come on. Don't tell me you don't love that jade elephant," I teased.

Why were we talking about crap made in China? About junk food? The elephant we needed to talk about was the one in the room: Robinson's *blood*, his *illness*, which wasn't a matter of nutrition.

On the other hand, ignoring that truth was exactly how we'd gotten as far as we had. We didn't sit around and mope. We took charge; we took *off*. We laughed and we drove too fast and we stuck our heads out the window and gave cancer the finger. Because we understood that a person could be dead long before they actually died. And no matter what the future held for us, we didn't ever want to be that kind of people.

Robinson blinked drowsily. "I do kind of like the elephant. I think jade's supposed to be good luck. We could probably use a little of that."

His voice was thick with sleep. His eyes closed, and he leaned his head on my shoulder. I squeezed his fingers, still wrapped in mine. Just like he'd said, we were in this together.

"Everything's going to be fine," I whispered. But Robinson had fallen asleep already, and he couldn't hear me lie.

27

THE BITTER IRONY OF MY LIFE WAS THAT two years after my sister, Carole Ann, died in a pediatric oncology ward in Portland, Oregon, I became a patient in the same wing. I recognized all the nurses, who'd shaken their heads in disbelief. "Both Moore babies?" they'd whispered. *"Both?"*

If God or fate or karma has decided you're going to get cancer, though, you cross your fingers for a kind like mine. Hodgkin's lymphoma is not uncommon, which means that doctors know a lot about it, and by now they're pretty good at curing it. That's the glass half-full.

"Yeah, the glass half-full...of shit," Robinson used to say. I'd met him for the first time in that place, and every time he'd curse, I'd sort of punch him in the arm, because I didn't like it. But I did like *him*, which made being there a little bit easier.

Don't get me wrong. Even a highly curable cancer is no walk in the park. Yes, the hospital walls were painted pretty colors, the nurses wore Winnie-the-Pooh scrubs, and some of the older kids pretended the ward was a boarding school complete with uniforms of thin blue gowns, fuzzy slippers, and bald heads covered in colorful scarves. But being there and being sick totally sucked.

Until the day I met Robinson. Until the day he found me.

If life were a movie, we'd have had what they call a "meet cute." Sort of like this: I'd knock into Robinson while carrying a giant stack of magazines I'd borrowed from the waiting room. And all those good, trashy weeklies like *Us*, *People*, and *Life & Style* would slide everywhere on the floor. I'd make a joke about studying for my pop culture quiz, and he'd laugh as he helped me pick up the mess. By the time the magazines were back in my arms, we'd have realized we were totally hot for each other, and hilarity and romance would ensue for the next ninety minutes.

In real life, it went like this: in a narcotic haze from a bad reaction to a chemo treatment, I was staring at the TV, convinced that Barney the purple dinosaur was speaking directly to me. When I failed to decipher his message, I fell asleep, waking later to see a beautiful dark-haired boy sitting next to my bed. I knew then that I had died, because unless I had been

transported to heaven, there was no way a guy that hot was smiling at me.

But I wasn't dead. It was Robinson, and he was real. He said to me, "You look like shit. I feel like shit. Let's be friends."

And just like that, we were. That's how magnetic Robinson was: he could tell you that you looked terrible, and you'd still adore him.

Robinson was sicker than I was, but he didn't act like it. He had a rare kind of non-Hodgkin's lymphoma called Burkitt's. The *non* means it's worse.

"Burkitt was the doctor who discovered the cancer in equatorial Africa," Robinson informed me. "It's a lot more common there." He sounded almost proud of his strange and exotic cancer. Then he grinned. "Burkitt also had this whole elaborate theory about the right posture for taking a crap. He said if you squatted—you know, like a baseball catcher—you'd never get colon cancer. Seriously, you can't make this stuff up."

I looked up Burkitt's immediately. For patients with Robinson's numbers (his cancer was Stage IV) the survival rate was 50 percent.

There were kids on the ward who'd only have to have a foot amputated or a mysterious lump removed, and then they'd live to be a hundred. Why Robinson? Why this disease? But Robinson was philosophical. He said, "Fifty percent? I've seen worse."

We all had.

A 50 percent chance of surviving was a flip of a coin. So the night after I learned what the odds for him were, I sat up in my adjustable hospital bed, held a penny tight in my palm, and squeezed my eyes shut. "Heads, he lives," I said. I didn't even whisper what tails meant. I threw the penny into the air, and when I caught it, I had to breathe deeply for a long time before I could look.

It was heads.

I can't tell you how much weight I put on that coin toss. I believed in it with every single cell of my body. *Our luck would not run out.* That's what I told myself.

But they were only words. My mom could predict rain by the dull ache in her knee. My childhood dog, Sadie, could sense the mailman when he was still two blocks away. In this weird, quiet way, they knew what was coming.

And now, so did I.

Now, in the cold, cold waiting room, Robinson leaned against me. I could feel his breath. I imagined I could see the faint, precious pulse of his heartbeat, fluttering beneath the skin. He was so beautiful, so alive.

But for how long? I didn't need a doctor to tell me what I already knew. Robinson—my better self, my heart, my life— was very possibly dying.

Our luck would not run out? *Please*, Axi. Everything runs out eventually. *Everything.*

28

EVENTUALLY, ROBINSON WAS ADMITTED
to the La Junta hospital, and a nurse took us to a private room.
She helped him into a bed, and I hopped up on the empty one
beside him.

"Are you going to write this down?" Robinson wondered
aloud. "In your journal?"

"I only write down the good parts of our adventures," I
said.

Robinson snorted. "You can't write a book without a con-
flict."

I said, "Who said anything about a book? This is my journal. It's a pink notebook I got at Walgreens for two-ninety-nine."

Robinson shrugged. "You never know…"

For some reason, this made me laugh. "Sure, I'll write a

book," I told him, "as long as you promise to actually read it."

He held up his little finger. "Pinkie swear."

But before I could lean toward him, a voice boomed from the doorway. "So—just what do we have here?" We looked up to see a bearded giant wearing a lab coat and staring at us.

He introduced himself as Dr. Ellsworth, and he hadn't even asked Robinson's last name before he launched into a list of questions. Did Robinson use drugs? Alcohol? Had he traveled internationally recently? Had he ever had an ulcer? Was he allergic to any foods? Had he eaten any spinach during last month's *E. coli* outbreak?

Robinson shuddered at the thought of spinach. He answered no to everything.

I was still amazed by the doctor's size. He could have been a circus strongman, but now he was bending over Robinson's chest, listening to his heart and lungs.

He was frowning.

He palpated Robinson's stomach, and Robinson inhaled sharply, wincing. I had to look away then. I couldn't bear to see him in pain.

After several minutes, Dr. Ellsworth spoke. "I'm going to send you to get a CT scan and an X-ray. There are…abnormalities."

Just because I was expecting to hear something like this didn't mean it didn't knock the wind out of me. I drew in a wobbly breath as Robinson said, "Actually, if it's all the same to you, Doctor, I'd rather not have those things."

"You might be a very ill young man," the doctor said.

Robinson watched him, blinking his dark eyes. "Might," he allowed. "But let's just leave it at that. No news is good news, right? In the meantime, I do think I have a touch of the flu or something." He offered the best rakish grin he could muster, which, considering the situation, was pretty impressive.

"You have walking pneumonia," Dr. Ellsworth said. "And pleurisy is likely. I can tell you that right now."

"Please let that be all he has," I whispered. I suddenly thought of the orb Robinson had bought me in Mount Shasta, and I reached for it at the bottom of my backpack. I ran my fingers over its smooth surface. It was both a worry stone and a good-luck charm.

The doctor turned to me. "And you?" he asked. "Are you in need of any medical care you'd like to refuse?"

I shook my head. "I'm just here for moral support," I said.

Dr. Ellsworth walked over to the side of the bed I was borrowing and touched my neck. His fingers were cool. "I see the scar right here," he said. "It's from a radiation burn, isn't it?"

I moved away from his touch, saying nothing. I wasn't a patient here, and I didn't have to answer. It didn't matter what I'd had. I was clear. In remission.

Although, as my dad's friend Critter used to say, *Just because it's sunny today don't mean the shitstorm ain't comin'.*

Dr. Ellsworth crossed his arms over his massive chest.

165

"What's going on with you two?" he asked. "Where did you come from?"

Robinson and I looked at each other. He shook his head almost imperceptibly.

I spoke for us. "We can't say at the moment."

Dr. Ellsworth gave us both sharp looks. "This is not a game. It is my belief that this young man here has a mass in his abdomen. A tumor. Do you comprehend the seriousness of that?"

Robinson tried to sit up. "Hey, Axi. What's the difference between a doctor and a lawyer?"

I knew this joke—it was one of Robinson's standards. And I was only half-surprised he was trotting it out now. Playing along, I said, "I don't know. What?"

"A lawyer will rob you; a doctor will rob you and kill you, too."

Dr. Ellsworth made a sound in his throat—a choked-back laugh? A grunt of annoyance? "I'm trying to help," he said.

"Then bring in a TV," Robinson quipped. "Preferably one with cable."

The truth was, Robinson and I had a routine down. We'd perfected it in the halls of the Portland cancer ward. The nurses loved us. We were the Abbott and Costello of cancer. "Hey, Robinson," I said. "What do you call a person who keeps getting lymphoma over and over again?"

"I don't know—what?" But he was already laughing.

"A lymphomaniac!" I cried.

Robinson whooped and pretended to slap his thigh. "Oooh, that was a good one," he said.

Dr. Ellsworth sighed. "If there were a drug to prevent gallows humor, I'd prescribe it for both of you." But I could tell that he thought we were just a tiny bit funny.

He stepped toward the door. "I'm going to give you some intravenous antibiotics, and I'm going to encourage you to think very hard about those tests I mentioned."

"I don't like tests," Robinson said. "I always fail them."

"Where are your parents, young man?"

I glanced at Robinson. That was a question whose answer I didn't know, either.

Robinson turned away. "I'm a legal adult," he said. "Do you want to check my ID?"

Dr. Ellsworth gave Robinson one more long look, then shook his head and left the room.

Robinson closed his eyes. "I'm just going to take a little nap," he said. "If you can stand to be without my company for a while."

I got up and pulled the thin blanket over him. I didn't want him to leave me, not even for a minute. "I think I can manage," I said softly.

He said, "You should close your eyes, too."

"I'm not tired," I said, lying again. But I knew I couldn't sleep, anyway; I needed to watch him. To make sure he didn't start coughing again. To make sure the blood stayed inside him, where it was supposed to be. To watch his chest rise and fall, rise and fall.

I sat down by his bedside. I hoped the antibiotics would work their invisible cellular magic, and quickly. And I wished that what Robinson needed was only—to use his terminology—a little tune-up. Because we weren't going to stick around to get six weeks of chemo in La Junta. That wasn't in the plan.

A few minutes later, I looked up to see that Dr. Ellsworth had returned. "We're moving you to a different room," he said. "I don't want you too far from a ventilator. Or the nurses' station."

Robinson looked over at me and offered a faint, sleepy smile. "Precautionary, of course," he said.

"Of course," I repeated. "You just have a touch of whatever's been going around." Like cancer was contagious, the way doctors once thought it was. Like it was no more serious than the common cold.

I didn't dare look at Dr. Ellsworth. He was going to add *crazy* to Robinson's list of diagnoses, I could already tell. And that was just fine with me.

Because as far as I knew, nobody ever died of crazy.

29

IN THE EVENING THEY SEDATED Robinson, because his breathing had become labored and painful. That, apparently, was the pleurisy. Or maybe it was the pneumonia. I didn't want to know. When they said things like "peritoneal fluid analysis" and "low platelet count," I put my fingers in my ears.

Alone, I read every magazine I could find: *Golf Digest, Sport Fishing,* and *Fit Pregnancy.* None held any useful information for me, but considering I'm a golf hater, a vegetarian, and a virgin, that was not exactly surprising.

Then I wandered the corridors, noticing again how much one hospital resembles another. They sound the same (the beeps of heart monitors, the hiss of oxygen machines, the murmuring tones of visitors). They serve the same food (syrupy, too-sweet grape juice; soggy dinner rolls; and pink, plastic-looking ham).

They even smell the same (odors of disinfectant, recycled air, and bodies and what comes out of them—a mix I can only describe as *lavatorial*).

As terrible as La Junta General was, a tiny part of me relaxed a little. Unlike the rest of our cross-country journey, the hospital ward was known territory. A place I could navigate. And I guess I was glad to have a roof over my head again.

But as Robinson would be the first to point out, you can't be Bonnie and Clyde in a hospital. You're in a different movie altogether.

"Pace much?" one of the nurses asked with a friendly smile when I walked by the station for the twentieth time.

I smiled. "Sorry. Just stretching my legs."

"No worries, keep at it," she said. "Exercise does a body good."

She looked like she could stand to get a little exercise herself, but she was busy playing FreeCell on her computer. Slow night in the ER, I guess.

I turned down a new hallway and came upon a set of heavy double doors. Pushing them open, I found myself in the foyer of a small chapel.

It was utterly unlike the rest of the sterile white hospital. The front wall was a deep red. There was a plain wooden altar with LED candles flickering alongside it. There was no statue of Jesus on the cross, though—no Mary or Ganesh or Buddha or L. Ron Hubbard, either, or whoever it was people prayed to around here. There was just that red—the red of valentines, of

blood. Faint classical music came from invisible speakers.

I sat down on a bench. My parents had taken me to church about three times before they lost interest in shushing Carole Ann and me every other second. Now I was the only one in the room, so I didn't quite know what to do with myself. I put my face in my hands. Anyone who poked a head in would think I was praying.

I thought of Carole Ann and Robinson—and myself, too. How we'd all been affected by forces that felt terrifying and supernatural but were actually just terrifying and basic. Cancer is abnormal cells dividing without control and invading other tissues. It's that simple. But it was still always a mystery: *Why in the hell is my body trying to kill me?*

Before I went into remission, I hated my body for betraying me. And considering that I was being treated for cancer at the same time I was suddenly growing breasts and having to shave my legs and stick giant pads in the crotch of my underwear—well, it felt like my body was adding insult to injury.

Having Robinson with me on that journey meant everything. We were able to laugh at how weak we were. We had contests over who had the worst mouth sores (chemo causes them; they're awful). We goaded each other to eat food when food was the last thing we wanted.

We'd saved each other, Robinson and me. Or at least, he had saved me.

But why me? Why was I doing so well when Robinson was so sick? When Carole Ann was dead?

What I know about sickness—beyond the fear, the uncertainty, and the nightmarish drudgery of it—is that it builds a wall between the sick and the well. Back in the pediatric oncology ward, Robinson and I had been on the same side of that wall. Now I couldn't bear the idea of any wall between us. I wanted to experience what he was experiencing. I wanted to be with him. For everything.

In a way, I felt like my body was betraying me again—but

this time, it was killing me by keeping me well. I knew that wasn't rational. It wasn't like I wanted to get cancer again... right?

I stared at the flickering lights for a long time. When no priest or angel or epiphany from above came to answer my question, I decided to go back to Robinson.

He was getting the intravenous antibiotics for his chest infection. They'd given him morphine, too, because otherwise the medicine hurt too much going in.

Robinson turned toward me and smiled. His eyelids were heavy, his skin pale. "Have I ever told you how beautiful you are?" he asked.

I straightened the edge of his blanket. "That's the morphine talking," I said.

But still I blushed. And I hoped and prayed that it was really him talking.

30

I WAS STANDING ON THE EDGE OF THE cliff again, and dream-Robinson was beside me, holding my hand. I knew he was supposed to tell me something that would reassure me, but he was so silent he could have been a ghost.

I took a step forward, about to plummet into the depths—

I woke with a start.

In the darkness, there was soft rock playing from the radio at the nurses' station, a kind of music that Robinson liked to claim was as deadly as cancer. The nurses always had a good laugh at that one.

I was about to close my eyes and roll back over when I saw the shape at the side of my bed. *Robinson*. He moved forward and touched my shoulder. Even in the darkness, I could see that he had his clothes on—not a hospital gown. "Axi?"

I pushed myself up.

"It's time to leave," he said softly.

He placed my backpack at the foot of my bed and held out his hand to help me up. His fingers were warm and reassuring, as if I were the sick one. Robinson was always so careful with me. I remembered walking the long halls of the Portland hospital with him, the two of us so weak we shuffled like octogenarians.

"Octo-what?" he'd said.

"Octogenarians. People in their eighties."

He'd laughed. "Oh, I don't have to worry about living that long."

I'd stopped in my tracks. What about that coin toss? Didn't that mean anything? "What are you talking about?" I'd demanded.

Robinson grinned. "Axi, I'm going to be a rock star—I'll wear out my body by sixty-five," he explained. "Too many decibels. Too much rock 'n' roll. You can read about me in books someday. I'll be the guy slayed by music. *I knew that dude*, you'll say. *He was cool.*"

Now, in the middle of the night, in the middle of nowhere, I touched Robinson's shoulder. "Are you sure you're okay?"

Faintly, I could see him smile. "I think I've seen enough of La Junta," he said. "We'd better be moving on."

31

I DIDN'T BOTHER ASKING HIM TO LOOK away while I changed into ever-so-slightly-less-grimy clothes. For one, it was dark, and for two, what secrets did I still have from him?

Besides the fact that I loved him, obviously. But maybe it was time to let go of that secret, too, if only I could be brave enough.

Robinson had moved over to the window, his face dimly lit by the orange glow of the parking lot lights. When I was dressed in my jeans and a rumpled sweater, I went to stand beside him.

"Did you know that Cancer is the dimmest constellation of the zodiac?" he asked.

When I shook my head, he pointed to the dark sky. "It's over there. And it doesn't look anything like a crab."

"I didn't know you were such an astronomer."

Out of the corner of my eye I could see his grin. "Axi, I have facets you can't even imagine."

I felt almost dizzy when he said that. Is it possible that you can love someone more than you love life itself, and yet you're still never going to know for sure everything he's thinking? I wanted—I needed—to see every facet of Robinson that I could, for as long as I could.

"And the crazy thing?" Robinson went on. "Every star that you see out there is bigger and brighter than the sun. They only look small because they're farther away." He was still gazing out the window as if a message were written for him in the sky.

The message is right here, Robinson, I wanted to say. *Look at me, and I'll tell you.*

Still, though, I was mute. I tentatively moved closer to his side and clumsily knocked into him with my hip. For a moment I worried the bump I'd given him was too hard. How fragile was he? But when he didn't seem to notice, I wondered if I should try it again. I wondered if I should grab his hand. I wondered if I should tackle him, throw him to the floor, and kiss every inch of his frail, beautiful body.

I scooted closer to him again, and this time it felt like it registered. He was suddenly more aware of me. He stayed very still as energy seemed to ripple in the air between us. I held my breath, and I think he was holding his, too.

Now is the time, Axi, I thought. *Carpe diem.*

I reached across him to his far hand and turned him toward me. "I have something to tell you," I whispered.

"I'm all ears," he whispered back.

He waited silently, giving my eyes time to search his face: his high forehead, his deep-set eyes, his full mouth.

I opened my lips, but nothing came out. I was the writer, the reader—and now, when I truly needed to say the things I'd been wanting to say for what seemed like forever, words were utterly failing me.

"It's okay," Robinson said softly.

What's okay? I could have asked. *Nothing is okay! We're in a hospital because you could be dying! How many more chances will I have to chicken out before you're suddenly gone?*

If I couldn't say anything, I had to do something. Right this second. Or I might never get to feel the sensation of his lips touching my lips.

I couldn't live without that.

And that was all it took. I wrapped my arms around his neck and brushed my face so close to his that his unshaven chin tickled my skin. And then—I kissed him.

When our lips met, in a rush of warmth and softness, electricity flooded my body. I was sure that I began to glow. That I was full of starlight.

Finally. This was what I'd been aching for. And from the way Robinson's breath instantly melted into mine...I felt for all the world like he'd been aching for it, too.

Why on earth had we waited so long?

Robinson's arms tightened around my waist, and his hands found their way into my hair. A tiny moan escaped from his throat, and he kissed me full-strength, like he'd never been sick and never would be again...like he was more alive than ever.

And so was I.

After a minute, or an hour, we pulled apart, breathless. My cheeks were burning, and my whole body felt like it was vibrating. Like it was singing.

At first Robinson's eyes looked so solemn that my breath caught in my throat. Then, like a light blinking on in the darkness, came the smile that I craved, that crooked grin full of life.

"I love you, Axi Moore," he whispered. "What else can I say?"

I shook my head and smiled, my eyes glistening. I was still so overwhelmed that I couldn't say a word.

If this was what life was like without words—a life of *doing*, not just talking—I just might be willing to give them up forever.

32

IT WAS TIME TO GO. WE HURRIED OUT
into the darkness, Robinson's arm wrapped around my
shoulders. It was like a hug—as if now that we'd finally really
touched, we couldn't bear to let go of each other—but it was
also him using me to hold himself up.

I was still glowing. I felt brighter than any of the stars.

Kissing Robinson was like coming to the end of the desert and finding a spring. It was sunshine after years of winter.
It was Christmas in June. It was—oh, give me a break, why
bother with dumb poetic phrases?

What I felt was joy.

Joy that totally swept away the anxiety of breaking out of a
hospital against medical advice. My list of rebellious feats was
growing longer by the second.

At the edge of the parking lot, Robinson leaned down

and gave me another deep kiss. Then he pulled away, smiling. "Suddenly I feel like I can do anything," he said.

I felt exactly the same way. Everything would be fine. Or even better than fine. Magical. "Just tell me that *anything* doesn't include taking a different car," I said, pressing my hand against his scratchy cheek. "This is excitement enough."

Robinson kissed me again, his lips soft but urgent. At this rate, we'd never leave the parking lot—and maybe I didn't even care, as long as this kept happening.

"I'd never ditch Chuck the Truck," Robinson said after a while. "He needs to see Detroit."

I laughed giddily—clearly the making out was messing with my head a little. "Chuck the Truck?"

"Yes, ma'am," Robinson said. "Second cousin to Charley the Harley."

He laughed at his own joke and climbed into the truck. He started the engine, revving it a few times to warm it up. Then, for some reason, he scooted over into the passenger seat, where I was about to sit.

I quit my giggling. "Um, Robinson?" I said, eyeing the empty space behind the steering wheel.

He leaned back against the headrest. "Yeah, I know I said I felt like I could do anything…but I think it's probably better if you drive right now."

I noticed that his voice had become raspy again, and he had his hand over his chest, as if he were having trouble breathing.

"Then we should turn around and go back to the hospital!" I insisted. "Detroit will still be there in a couple of days."

Robinson shook his head. "No way, Axi. I'm done with that place."

"But what if it's not done with you?"

He patted the seat. "Come here, Axi. Sit beside me."

I went around to the other side and clambered onto the truck's high bench seat. Robinson put his arm around my shoulders, and I buried my face in his flannel shirt. It smelled like the hospital, but underneath that, like him. Like soap and pine and *boy*.

Of course I wanted to leave. I wanted to be alone with Robinson again. I wanted more of what we'd started in the hospital. A *lot* more.

But was this a mistake?

When Robinson spoke again, his voice seemed stronger. It also seemed like he'd been reading my thoughts. "Who cares if leaving here is a mistake? I'd make this mistake again, a million times," he insisted. "We're together. That's what matters. I want to take this trip with you. That's all I want. That's all I need. I'm not going to be irradiated or scanned or biopsied or whatever it is they want to do to me."

I spoke into his shirt because I didn't want to move away from him, not even a single millimeter. "But what if it's a death sentence? To refuse treatment now?" I whispered.

Robinson scoffed. "A hospital is a death sentence. You can cut your finger, get a staph infection, and the next thing you know, you're checking out the grass from underneath. Leaving now, Axi, is choosing life."

I could hear the quick beating of his heart. "But what if it's a shorter life?"

He shrugged. "Well, as Kurt Cobain said, 'It's better to burn out than to fade away.' Although, actually, he was quoting a Neil Young song."

I sat up suddenly. What in the world was I going to do with this infuriating person? "May I remind you that Cobain used it in his *suicide note*?"

"Well, you have to admit he had a point, GG," Robinson said mildly.

I closed my eyes and breathed in deeply, calming myself. Robinson's hand reached out, and his fingers slipped between mine, trying to reassure me.

What if doing what you wanted and doing what was right seemed like two entirely different things? What if by living the life you chose, you somehow doomed yourself—or worse, someone you loved?

After a minute, I opened my eyes. We couldn't know the future or how long it would last. We could only choose to be happy and alive right now.

"Okay, okay, you win, Robinson," I said. "But only on these conditions." I held up two fingers. "One: do not call me GG, remember? Two: you are not allowed to die. Do you hear me?"

Robinson grinned and saluted me. "Yes, ma'am," he said. "Agreed. Ten-four. Et cetera."

We shook on it, as if it were just that simple.

And then I gritted my teeth and started driving.

33

Robinson fell asleep almost
immediately. This was fine with me, because I needed complete
and total focus on my new assignment: piloting a speeding
death-and-dismemberment trap across the country.

Because, FYI, car crashes kill way more kids than cancer
does. Those crosses you see on the side of the highway, the
little white ones hung with fading silk flowers? They're for
people my age. ("People who were texting," my dad liked to
remind me—because he never wanted to blame Budweiser for
anything.)

I managed not to become a highway statistic in those early
hours, but there were occasional...problems. For instance, I
pulled into a Texaco for gas but didn't know how to oper-
ate the pump, and Robinson was sleeping so deeply I couldn't
wake him. After I begged some nice old man to help me fill my

tank, I got back on the highway going in the wrong direction. For thirty miles.

After I turned around, I tried playing the radio softly. It barely worked, so I turned it off and had only my thoughts to keep me company:

I never knew how damn big *the United States is.*

Where's the nearest Starbucks?

How come my dad hasn't found me yet?

The miles ticked by, monotonous but nerve-racking. Eventually, I just started talking out loud to keep myself company.

"Don't take this the wrong way," I said, though I knew Robinson was still in dreamland, "but I don't think I ever believed we'd make it this far. Like, wouldn't my dad call the cops when he woke up and found me gone? Or even just call Critter? That guy's a human bloodhound."

Critter had even found the diamond that had fallen out of my mom's engagement ring—in a river. Not that having the diamond back encouraged her to stick around.

"Obviously, I'm not saying I want to be caught. I want to keep going. But I guess I wonder if we've just been really lucky so far? Or is there a certain amount of…disinterest on my dad's part concerning the location of his remaining daughter?"

I took a sip of cold truck-stop coffee. It felt good to talk about it, even if—or especially because—Robinson wasn't listening.

"And then there's you," I said to Robinson's sleeping silhouette. "Where are your parents? Aren't they worried about you? Do they have any idea where you are?"

When I met Robinson on the cancer ward, he'd brushed off all talk of his family. No sad-eyed father sat with him while he got his chemo; no weeping mother held his hand while he was bombarded with radioactive particles.

He was, for all that the rest of us could see, 100 percent alone.

On the other hand, no one was more popular. Robinson could turn a Domino's delivery guy into his new BFF in five minutes. Once I heard two of the nurses talking about how they wanted to adopt him. And of course he could've had his pick of girls, on or off the ward. He was magnetic.

Out of everyone, he'd chosen me. I was his family.

When we were discharged, Robinson followed me to Klamath Falls. "We need to stick together, Axi," he'd said. "Plus, I have an uncle there. Says I can live in his basement."

I didn't question it—all I cared about was not saying good-bye.

I realized now how much he'd left behind in the course of his life: his parents, his uncle, the doctors who wanted to treat him. It was as if he'd run from everyone but me.

"Am I enough, Robinson?" I heard myself ask. "Can I really be everything you need?"

He shifted in his sleep, stretching out his long legs. But he didn't wake up to answer that critical question.

"I wonder," I went on, "if it's possible to go so far that I'll stop being afraid of us not ever coming back." I chewed on my lip for a while, then drank some more bitter coffee. "I thought I'd figured out the risks. I thought I had everything planned out. But I hadn't counted on you getting sick."

I sneaked another glance at him. His eyelashes made a dark curve against his pale cheek, and his left hand twitched, moving in a dream.

There was another thing I hadn't counted on. And that was falling in love, as fast and irrevocably as you would fall off a cliff, and realizing that loving someone might mean to simultaneously want to slug them and hold them and possibly have to watch them die...I hadn't counted on that.

I reached over and touched his cheek. "I love you," I whispered. "Please stay with me."

In his sleep, Robinson turned and sighed.

34

Robinson and I stood, our fingers intertwined, and stared at the ruins: crumbling buildings, burned-out houses, litter-strewn sidewalks, and the empty hulk of an old Ford factory.

"Welcome to Detroit," Robinson said happily. He was feeling much better today, and I was hoping our location had nothing to do with it. "Motor City. Motown. I could have been stuck growing up here if my parents hadn't left."

"It was probably a little nicer back when they were growing up here, huh," I said, all the while hoping it wasn't symbolic that the first place Robinson and I visited together as a couple (because that's what we were now, right?) was in total shambles.

With the tip of his boot, Robinson sent an empty can of Red Bull arcing into the summer air. "Yeah, probably it was."

I took a picture of a mildewed sofa with a bunch of pigeons perched on it. To our left, a tree was growing out of the side of a building.

"I guess it could be beautiful, in a way, if you were into romantic decay or steampunk or something," I said. "Or maybe we should imagine it like the Parthenon in Greece. A bunch of grand old ruins."

Robinson nodded thoughtfully. "That old Ford factory is where my grandma and grandpa met and fell in love," he said. "On the assembly line." He gestured off vaguely in another direction. "And down that way was the Chrysler plant where my mom and dad did the same thing."

I bent down and plucked a dandelion from a crack in the

pavement. "So I guess this used to be a pretty romantic place then," I said.

Robinson was quiet, gazing out on the desolation. Thinking, maybe, about his family, wherever they were. So it took me completely by surprise when he whirled me toward him. He held me close for a moment, his arms tightening around me. And then he bent down and kissed me, long and deep, until I felt that familiar softening inside, my legs going wobbly. Like maybe if he didn't keep holding me up, I might dissolve.

When he pulled away, he smiled. "What do you mean *used to be?*"

I kept my arms around his waist. I wanted to be as close to

him as possible, for as long as possible. "I stand corrected," I said, looking up at him, backlit by the sun, so the ends of his dark hair looked like they were on fire. "Two generations of your family fell in love here. That's pretty amazing." Thinking: *Now three.*

He nodded, but he didn't elaborate. His eyes had that far-away look in them again.

"I guess you come by your car obsession naturally, then," I continued. I wanted him to keep talking, because he was always so tight-lipped about his family that I knew almost nothing about them.

"My dad always said his first baby was his 1967 Mustang," Robinson offered.

"So you grew up here?" I asked.

Robinson began to whistle that Sufjan Stevens song about Detroit.

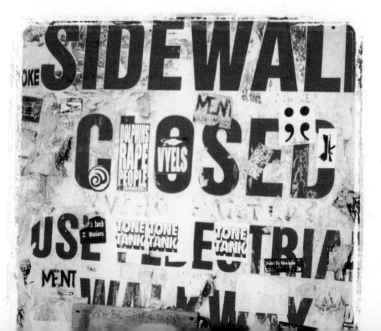

I jabbed him in the ribs. "Seriously, you're not going to answer? You tell me you love me, but you don't want to tell me where you were freaking born?" I was laughing, but I was a little offended, too.

When Robinson looked down at me again, his face was clouded. "I'm just not…in close touch with my parents these days. It makes me sad to think about them. So I try not to."

Seeing as how he'd had enough hardship lately, I decided not to press the issue. "Just give me a natal city."

Robinson smiled. "You and your fancy words. *Natal.* World, I ask you: who says *natal* besides Alexandra Jane Moore?"

I jabbed him in the ribs again. There wasn't anyone but pigeons to answer him.

"No, I wasn't born here," Robinson said finally. "Chrysler moved the plant before I was born. My parents went to North Carolina, and that's where I showed up. My dad worked for a steel company for a while, and then he opened up his own auto repair shop." Robinson began to whistle some other song I didn't recognize, ending our conversation.

I sighed. "At this rate, it'll take me fifty years to learn about your childhood."

He reached out and touched my cheek with his fingertips. "Oh, Axi-face, who cares about the past? We have now."

"Axi-face?" I repeated. I took his hand and brought his fingers to my lips. Smiling, I kissed them on their tips, one after the other.

He nodded. "It's new. You like it?"

196

"I'll get back to you on that." The truth was, I'd like any pet name he came up with. But I wasn't going to admit it.

For a while we just stood there, being quiet with each other, our fingers touching lightly. We watched birds circling overhead, and the clouds shifting. It struck me then that the earth could be covered in trash and wreckage, but you could always find something that seemed clean and perfect. Maybe that was a metaphor for something.

After a while I leaned in to give Robinson a gentle kiss. He took my face in his hands. "So," he said, "can I buy you dinner or what?"

I smiled. "Does that make it a date?"

Grinning back, he shrugged. "Depends. Am I going to get past first base?"

"Pig," I said, laughing.

"Pig!" he repeated. "Speaking of which, let's go eat some."

35

WE PLAYED MOTOWN IN THE CAR—
Diana Ross, Stevie Wonder—as we drove downtown. Robinson
hummed and tapped his fingers on the dash, following the
drumbeats and adding little flourishes of his own.

We found a restaurant full of Christmas lights and orange-
velvet banquettes, its walls hung with funky instruments and
dozens of black-and-white pictures of Detroit in its old-timey
heyday. Someone was playing the piano in the corner, loudly,
and the place was packed.

"It's like a speakeasy crossed with a TGI Fridays," I said as
we sat down.

"Or, like, if Liberace were a gangster and this was his living
room."

"Or it's the hangout of a pimp who likes jazz and antiques,"
I said.

Robinson grinned. "It's awesome."

We found a table in the corner, and the waiter came by and set two small glasses full of clear liquid on the table. "Hungarian moonshine," he said, by way of greeting. "It's Ed's birthday." He seemed to think we should know who Ed was. "I'll be back to take your order in a minute."

Robinson and I looked at the glasses and then at each other. "Should we?" I asked.

He pretended to look disappointed. "I have so many fake IDs. I really wanted the chance to use another one."

We held up our glasses and clinked them together. "*Sláinte*," I said.

"*Slan-cha?*" Robinson said, frowning. "I've heard that before...what does it mean?"

I shrugged. "Dunno. It's just some old Irish toast." But of course I knew exactly what it meant. It meant "health." Because didn't that matter more than just about anything these days?

We knocked our glasses back, and the liquid burned down my throat, making me shudder. "Is that what radiator fluid tastes like?"

Robinson was sloshing it around in his mouth. Then he swallowed. "This is more like rubbing alcohol, I'd say."

I could feel it in my stomach now, warming me. Was it

possible that I felt looser, almost light-headed already? "Funny how a tiny little shot makes me feel so rebellious, when I'm already a car thief."

"I believe your term was *borrower*," Robinson noted.

"Because that's going to go over really well with the judge," I said. *"Oh, you were only borrowing that Porsche? No problem, then!"*

"You guys aren't from around here, are you?"

Robinson and I both looked up, startled. Guilty people are jumpy people, I guess. But it was only our waiter, who looked like he'd had a shot or two of the moonshine himself.

"No, sir," Robinson said, polite as can be.

The waiter pointed a finger at us. "Well, when you go back home, tell your friends how the Big D is doing just fine. I know you went and saw the closed-up factories; everybody does. But don't remember just the dead stuff. Remember this." He waved his arm around the happy, noisy room. "Remember the music and the moonshine. Is that a deal?"

Robinson and I nodded in tandem, and the waiter nodded back, satisfied. "Be back in a minute for that order."

When he left again, Robinson reached for my hand. "He's right. You have to remember the good stuff, Axi."

There was something about the way he said it that made a chill crawl up my spine. Like he was talking about much more than just Detroit. But I smiled and shook his hand anyway. "It's a deal. Scout's honor," I said. "Pinkie swear. Blah blah blah."

Robinson smiled. "You really are beautiful, you know that?" he said.

I looked down at the tabletop, but he reached out and tucked a finger under my chin, tipping my face up so I had to look right into his dark eyes.

"I mean it. Someone should tell you that every single day of your life. And right now, it gets to be me."

"It's always going to be you," I whispered.

He smiled again. "Get over here."

I went around to his side of the booth—and I sat down in his lap. It surprised both of us.

"Axi," he said, his voice soft and throaty. He ran a fingertip along my collarbone. "I never took you for the PDA type."

I shivered under his touch and pressed my forehead to his. When I spoke, our lips were tantalizingly close. "I'm learning how to live dangerously," I said.

He moved a fraction of an inch closer, so his lips almost brushed mine. "And what do you think of it?" he whispered.

I could almost taste him, and I held out for another long, delicious moment before finally pressing my mouth against his. Pushing my fingers into the tangle of his hair. We kissed, and warmth flooded my body.

"I like it," I whispered. "A lot."

I was nearly dizzy. *So this is what being intoxicated feels like.* But it wasn't from the shot I'd taken.

I am here to say that moonshine has nothing on love— and lust.

36

"The Blue Streak, the Mean Streak, and the Millennium Force," Robinson said. "I want to go on all of them. You only get to go on the Mean Streak, Axi."

He was pretending to be mad at me because I'd told him he couldn't have a Slim Jim until he'd eaten a banana. *Who are you, my mother?* he'd asked. I told him I couldn't watch him eat things made from mechanically separated chicken, aka *slimy pink meat paste*, anymore. Then he'd accused me of being a snotty vegetarian, and I had tackled and tickled him in the cab of the truck until he pleaded for mercy.

Now we were inside the gates at Cedar Point, the roller coaster capital of the world, nestled away in Sandusky, Ohio. Robinson, the daredevil, and me, the one who gets queasy on swings.

"I feel like the Junior Gemini might be more my speed," I said.

Robinson snorted. "Axi, you've done things lately that were

a whole lot scarier than a roller coaster." He cocked a finger at me, miming a gun.

"Don't remind me," I said.

"So. Shall we?" he asked, and held out his arm.

How could I refuse him? My scalawag, my partner in crime, my heart. He seemed like he was in perfect health. Was he? I didn't know, but now was the time to enjoy it.

We stood in the first line for an hour at least, surrounded by tired parents, their hyperactive eight-year-olds and sullen thirteen-year-olds, and a handful of sunburned retirees apparently willing to risk a heart attack to pull four g's on a single plummet.

Robinson saw me picking nervously at the hem of my T-shirt. "I'm telling you, this is going to be awesome," he said. "You're going to love it."

You must be
this tall
to ride alone

Unless
accompanied by
a responsible
person

He reached out and stroked my hair, and then his fingers moved down to my neck, kneading gently, reassuringly.

I almost moaned in pleasure. "Whatever you say..." Suddenly I wasn't thinking about the ride at all anymore. I was thinking about his hands. "Just keep doing that."

He laughed, rubbing my shoulders now, his body long and warm against my back. "Is this all it takes?" he asked. "A little back rub and tough Axi Moore turns into a quivering pile of acquiescence?"

"Ooh, that's a big word for you," I teased, trying to reclaim some measure of my sass. It wasn't easy.

"Maybe a good vocabulary is contagious," he said.

"Mmmmmmm."

"Although it seems like you might be losing yours."

"Mmmmm, lower…"

Robinson pulled me against him then, wrapping his arms around me from behind. "Maybe we shouldn't get too carried away," he said into my ear.

I sighed. "I guess…"

"But you're not afraid anymore, are you?"

I shook my head firmly. I wasn't.

Of course, my heart *did* begin pounding as soon as we climbed into the rear car of the Millennium Force, but I told myself it was because of excitement, not fear. I told myself that compared to all the things we'd done that were authentically dangerous, like stealing cars and riding motorcycles and breaking into people's pools, this was a walk in the park.

When we rose slowly up the hill, the tracks amazingly smooth beneath us, I grabbed Robinson's hand. Ahead of us people were already screaming. My knuckles went white around Robinson's fingers.

"Here it comes," he said.

When it seemed that the car could climb no higher into the faultless summer sky, we came to the top, paused for one silent, anticipatory second—and then plunged down. *Downdowndowndowndown.*

I screamed more loudly than I ever would have thought possible, and beside me Robinson let out a wild whoop of joy.

We raced and looped above the park, the wind making my eyes water and the car whipping me back and forth. I never stopped screaming, not for one single instant. And Robinson, he just laughed and laughed, letting my fingernails dig half-moons into his skin.

When we finally slowed down on the last approach and pulled under the awning to stop, I turned to Robinson, an enormous smile on my face. "Wow," I declared. "I want to do that again."

He gave me a triumphant look. "I knew you'd like it. I know you better than you know yourself." Then he reached up. "Give me a little help here, will you?"

I bent down and grabbed his hand, felt the weight of his palm in mine. "Thanks," he said. He brushed my bangs out of the way, and then his lips against my forehead were soft and sweet.

Holding hands loosely, we walked out onto the concourse, which was lined with flowers, streaming with people, and fragrant with the smells of fried food and sunscreen.

"Let's get cotton candy," I said.

"And sodas as big as our torsos," Robinson added.

"And nachos and licorice ropes," I cried, beginning to skip.

Robinson laughed as I tugged him along behind me. "I think the roller coaster knocked a screw loose. Don't you want some kale or something?"

"Tomorrow! Today we're going to act like normal teenagers!"

Because today I actually felt like one. As if nothing made Robinson and me different from anyone else our age—not sickness, crime, or anything. We were carefree. Lucky. Immortal.

"Have I ever told you I love you?" Robinson asked, catching up to me.

"Yes, but tell me again," I said, stopping to press myself against him.

"I love you," he said.

"I love you back," I said.

And then we kissed on the midway as crowds of people streamed around us and the roller coaster cars corkscrewed overhead.

37

"So," Robinson said, "onward to the
Big Apple?" We were finally heading for the truck, so exhausted
it felt like we ought to take turns carrying each other.

"No one calls it the Big Apple, you know," I said. "That's a
tourist thing."

"And we're not tourists?" he asked, lifting one dark eyebrow.

"No, we're *adventurers*," I said. "Explorers."

Robinson handed me the souvenir key chain he'd bought
at the last gift shop before the exit. It was a tiny model of the
Millennium Force, tucked inside a snow globe. "Since you're a
driver now and all," he said, grinning crookedly.

"Of course, I don't have any keys," I pointed out.

"Hey, if you don't want it, I can hook it to my screwdriver
or my cordless drill."

But of course I wanted it. It was a present from the boy I

loved. "I'm going to get you something, too, you know," I said, giving the snow globe a little shake.

Robinson demanded to know what it was, but I shook my head and mimed zipping my lips. "It's a surprise."

As I climbed into the driver's seat of the truck, I caught Robinson eyeing a sporty black BMW parked next to us. "Don't even think about it," I said. "I can't drive a stick."

"I'll teach you that next," he said. "And then, ATVs."

"Then dirt bikes," I said. "Why not?" Because everything was going to be just fine from now on. Maybe we really did have all the time in the world.

With Robinson as my navigator, I got us onto I-80. We had a long drive ahead of us, and the back roads just weren't going to cut it. I wanted something lined with Starbuckses.

"Doesn't time move slower the faster you go?" Robinson asked, staring out at flat green fields and signs for Pacific Pride truck stops.

I thought back to my physics class, which felt like it was about a million years ago (so what does that say about time?). "It's only a matter of nanoseconds or something. Time moves slower the closer you are to the earth, too."

"That gives me an excellent reason not to go mountain climbing."

"As if you needed one," I said.

"True. Somehow the thought of plunging hundreds of feet to my death never appealed to me." He toyed with the key chain, watching the snow sift down over the tiny roller coaster. "Do you ever think about what happens after?" he asked suddenly.

"After what?" I asked, moving into the passing lane.

"After we earn our wings," he said. He looked at me, waiting for a reaction.

I kept my eyes on the road. "Don't joke," I said.

Robinson crossed his arms over his chest. "I'm not joking. I'm asking."

"After we 'earn our wings'..."

"Don't you remember? Nurse Sophie used to say that all the time. She was totally sincere."

I pressed harder on the gas pedal. I was actually going the speed limit now. "Because she believed that when you die, you become an angel," I said. "Whereas you think we just take a dirt nap."

Robinson snickered. "Sorry. That dirt nap thing always gets me."

"It's not funny," I said.

But the truth was, we'd joked about death constantly back in the ward. All of us had, because somehow it made us less afraid. *Oh, I'm sooo tired*, someone would say, *I think I'll go sleep with the fishes*. Someone else would pipe up: *Lately I've been thinking about buying a pine condo*. Or: *Yeah, I'm planning on going into the fertilizer business*.

It was flipping Death the bird. And it made awful things like chemotherapy-induced nausea and hair loss just slightly less awful. But I thought—or hoped—that Robinson and I had left that sort of thing behind us. That such humor was no longer…medically relevant.

"I don't know, Robinson," I said, gripping the steering wheel. "I want to think there's something on the other side, but where's the evidence? No one sends you a postcard from the afterlife."

"Which is totally rude of them," he replied.

"I know, right?" I raised my fist. "Do you hear that, Carole Ann? *Rude.*"

Robinson reached over and put his hand on my knee. "Don't worry," he said. "I'll write you."

I felt like I'd been punched in the gut.

And I wanted to laugh, to show that I knew he was joking. But I wasn't entirely sure he was.

38

WE CROSSED THE WIDE EXPANSE OF Pennsylvania while Robinson slept. In the dark it looked like any other state, and I shot through it at seventy-five.

In East Orange, New Jersey, at midmorning, I sent Robinson into a Pathmark to buy groceries ("healthy stuff," I'd said, fully expecting him to try to pass off Froot Loops as actual fruit) while I went across the street to a place called All That Glitters Is Gold.

Thanks to my dad, I knew my way around a pawnshop. Which was how, for fifty bucks and the pearl-and-gold bracelet that had been my mother's, I bought Robinson an acoustic guitar.

"Where'd you go?" Robinson asked when I pulled up outside the Pathmark. He set the bag of groceries in the backseat, and

I was shocked to see an actual banana in it.

"Just a quick errand," I said, trying not to smile at the thought of the guitar hidden under the tent behind the backseat. "Did you honestly buy fruit and vegetables?"

He leaned over and kissed my neck. "Tell me where you went," he said, his lips ticklish on my skin.

I drew in my breath. "No." Every time he touched me, I felt my whole body begin to hum and shiver.

"Tell me," he said again, moving from my neck to my ear-lobe, his mouth light and teasing.

"Robinson," I whispered. I'd tell him anything, I'd give up

every secret I'd ever had, if he kept doing that.

I pulled him toward me, my mouth finding his. Before I knew it, my fingers were on the buttons of his shirt. I managed to get the top two undone, but then suddenly he moved away from me. He backed up against the car door, rebuttoning his shirt quickly.

I sat up straight, blinking. Confused. Didn't he want it, too?

"What?" I asked. "Why—"

"Security guards," Robinson said, nodding toward the burly guys walking up and down the rows of the parking lot.

There were three of them—two only a stone's throw away. But they could have been sitting in the backseat and I wouldn't have noticed while Robinson was filling up all my senses.

"We should probably go," he said. "We can, um, do some more of that later."

My cheeks were pink with embarrassment. "Okay," I said. As if I didn't want to shout, *Hell yes, we will!*

Robinson smiled. "But you know what? I think I want to drive."

I was so relieved that he was feeling good, so thrilled at the way I could kiss him now whenever I wanted—security guards notwithstanding—that I, small-town girl Axi Moore, didn't freak out at *all* when the New York skyline became visible along the turnpike, with its hills and valleys of silvery skyscrapers. I didn't care that we sat in traffic outside the

Holland Tunnel for forty-five minutes, or that Robinson got lost on the way across town to the East Village.

He was driving. He was happy and strong. That made everything okay.

39

TOGETHER, ALONG WITH A CRUSH OF tourists, we walked down St. Marks Place, trying on cheap sunglasses at the outdoor booths and browsing a two-story store called Trash and Vaudeville, where Robinson posed for a picture in a silver pleather biker jacket and I tried on a bright blue wig. We stopped into St. Mark's Bookshop, and I got a copy of Whitman's *Leaves of Grass* and a book of Dylan Thomas poems.

"Poetry?" Robinson said, looking aghast.

"Just read one," I said.

Robinson opened the Whitman to a random page and cleared his throat. "'A child said, What is the grass? fetching it to me with full hands; / How could I answer the child? . . . I do not know what it is any more than he. / I guess it must be the flag of my disposition, out of hopeful green stuff woven.'" He looked at me, intrigued. "Okay, I like that well enough. 'Hopeful green stuff woven.'"

I laughed. "I've got something you'll like better, though." I took his hand and led him down the street to the car.

"Is it my surprise?" he asked excitedly.

"Look under the tent," I said.

When Robinson pulled out the guitar, his whole face lit up. He hefted the weight of it in his hands and plucked a string experimentally.

"Axi, how—"

"Let's go play it," I said. I didn't want to have to tell him that I'd given up my mother's bracelet—the last thing I had of hers—to buy it. And that I wasn't the least bit sorry.

Hand in hand, we walked over to Tompkins Square Park and found a bench beneath a ring of gingko trees. Robinson strummed for a moment, finding the chords. They seemed familiar to me, but I didn't recognize the tune until he began to sing.

"Moving forward using all my breath," Robinson sang. The song was "I'll Melt with You."

I haven't talked about Robinson's voice, and this is partly because I can't explain it. It's clear and rough at the same time; it's intimate but also demands an audience. It's usually soft, but somehow you hear it not with just your ears but with your whole body. And with your heart most of all.

People who were walking by began to stop to listen as he sang. Robinson didn't seem to notice them gradually gathering

around him, though. His eyes were on his boot, tapping on the cobblestones. Every once in a while, he looked at me, right into my eyes, singing: *"I'll stop the world and melt with you…"*

Soon there was a big circle of people, young, old, and in between. Most of them were parents, with kids carrying stuffed bunnies or pockmarked Nerf footballs or—the older ones—iPhones. And these parents all knew the song, because it was the one they'd danced to thirty years earlier, when they were in high school and in love for the first time.

At first a few of them just mouthed the words, but then, quietly, they began to sing. Then others joined in, too, and they lost their hard, blank city faces and smiled, and in another minute it was a damn *sing-along*. I swear to God, there were people with tears in their eyes, because that's how beautiful Robinson is when he plays.

When the song ended, there was silence. For a moment I felt like the entire city went quiet and took one long, sweet breath. Like everyone, everywhere, was thinking about life, and how it is the happiest and saddest thing, the most wonderful and the most terrible and the most precious.

Then the silence broke. A woman in a bright yellow dress began to clap, and then, just the way the singing had grown, so did the clapping, until the applause was really loud. There was another woman blowing her nose, and a man staring up at the sky and blinking really hard and fast—but most people were just smiling.

An old man stepped forward and placed his cap on the ground. "You forgot to pass the hat," he said.

Robinson looked up, startled. "Pardon?" he said. He was still in the world of the song. He didn't realize there was anyone but him and me.

The old man looked a little like Ernie. He turned back to the crowd and called, "Cough it up for the young performer, all right?"

Robinson and I watched as almost every person stepped forward with quarters and dollars. I saw a woman give her daughter some money, and the girl tiptoed up and put a five into the hat. She was about Carole Ann's age when she died, the age she'd be forever. Her hair was even red, like my sister's.

"Thank you," I whispered.

Then it was all over, and the people left. Robinson and I were alone again. The hat was full of money.

Robinson was smiling at me. "We're rich," he said, and he pulled me onto his lap.

And truly, then, it felt like we were.

40

WE DECIDED TO SPLURGE ON A HOSTEL
that night. It sounded like a better idea than sleeping on a park
bench, though we would've had plenty of interesting company
had we gone that route.

The Grand Street Hostel was on the edge of Little Italy,
where it bleeds into Chinatown, and it looked decent enough
from the outside. There were a couple of backpacker types
smoking out front, and the guy at the desk was friendly in a
stoned sort of way.

But Robinson and I quickly learned that the difference
between a hostel and a hotel goes way, *way* beyond the minor
distinction in spelling. When the *s* is added, you subtract things
like privacy, comfort, and in this case, ceilings. The hostel was
a maze of tiny, thin-walled cells, sloppily constructed inside an
enormous hangarlike room.

"It's a bit more prison-y than I might have expected," Robinson said.

"No kidding," I agreed, stepping over a lone boot in the hall. "I feel like we should have gotten fingerprinted."

Luckily, we had our own room, with two single beds pushed right up against each other, and about six inches of floor space on either side.

"Well, the sheets look clean, at least," Robinson said brightly. Then he gave me a quick kiss and headed down the hall to the bathroom.

I sat on the corner of the bed and looked up at the non-ceiling. I could hear one end of an unpleasant cell phone conversation from a nearby room. *It's not my fault you got kicked out*, someone said. *Everyone's hated you for years.*

I hummed a little, trying to give this person some privacy. The song was "Tangled Up in Blue," but you wouldn't know it, since I can't carry a tune. I can't play an instrument, either. "It's okay," Robinson used to assure me. "You'll make me a great roadie someday."

I hummed faster and plucked at the corner of the sheet. I realized I was nervous, but also excited. Robinson and I hadn't been alone in a room together since LA, when we ever-so-chastely watched *Puss in Boots*. What would happen tonight, I wondered. How *un*chaste would we be?

This was another thing I definitely hadn't planned for. It was a road I'd just have to feel my way along.

No pun intended.

When Robinson came in from the bathroom, his hair was wet and he smelled like Ivory. His shirt hung loosely on his shoulders, and he was wearing blue plaid boxers.

He placed his folded jeans on top of his backpack. The bed sighed as he sat down.

"Hi," I half-whispered.

"Hi back," he said softly. "Well. What do you want to do now?"

I knew the answer to that question, even if it kind of...scared me a little. I took a deep breath, willing myself to be brave.

I slipped my shirt over my head.

Robinson sucked in his breath. And then he gently swept

225

the long waves of my hair away from the back of my neck and kissed me there. I shivered, goose bumps rising on my arms.

I could feel his breath, the impossible softness of his lips. I tilted my head back, and he ran a finger down my neck, stopping in the hollow of my clavicle for a moment before tracing each of my collarbones. He kissed along my shoulders, tickling me with the tiniest scratches of his unshaven chin.

We fell back against the bed, and above me, Robinson shrugged off his flannel. Then he bent his dark head down, and we were nothing but lips and tongues and teeth until we had to stop to catch our breath.

Then we lay there, our eyes locked in the half-light. Robinson was looking at me the way you'd look at something you'd lost a million years ago and never thought you'd find.

I gazed back at him in wonder, realizing how much of him there was still to discover: the scar on the inside of his palm, the blue veins in his wrist, the triangle of freckles on his chest, just to the left of his breastbone. These small, secret places. I wanted to know all of them.

But I didn't know how far things would go tonight. I wanted to be slow—and I wanted to go fast.

Robinson cleared his throat. "Do you—?" he began.

"I don't have any protection, if that's what you were going to ask." My voice came out too loud, and I shrank back against him in embarrassment.

He made a noise—a grunt? A half-laugh?

"I don't want to have kids," I blurted.

Then he really did laugh. "Whoa, Axi. Moving a little fast, are we?"

I pulled the blanket up over my face. This was all so new to me. Could I help it if I was doing it wrong?

But still, there was something I wanted him to know. I forced myself to keep talking, though part of me was ready to die of humiliation. "I didn't think we were about to make a baby, Robinson. I meant it as a philosophical thing. Between the Moore family cancer genes and, like, global warming, any kid of mine would be doomed. She'd be born with blue eyes and a ticking time bomb inside her, just like the rest of my

family. Talk about getting dealt a shitty hand of cards."

I tried not to sound as bitter as I felt.

Robinson was slowly stroking my fingers. "The blue eyes are so nice, though," he said quietly.

I smiled and placed my hand on his smooth chest. His arm was tucked under my neck, and as we lay there, it felt like we were extensions of each other. Like our bodies and our hearts had to be together to make one whole, perfect person.

41

THE NEXT MORNING WE WOKE UP IN
that same position—through some miracle, Robinson's arm
hadn't fallen asleep during the night. We got coffee and big,
pillowy bagels from a nearby bakery. We asked for them toasted
and dripping with butter—Robinson's favorite. Then we took
the subway up to the Metropolitan Museum of Art.

When a panhandler made his way through the subway car,
dressed as if it were winter instead of June, Robinson reached
into his pocket and produced a crumpled five.

The panhandler bowed as he accepted it. "Money and a
beautiful woman. You have everything, sir."

"Well, actually, now *you* have my money," Robinson
pointed out.

The panhandler considered this fact for a moment. "But
who needs money when you have her?"

"My thoughts exactly," Robinson said. He put his arm around me like I belonged to him.

When we got to the Met, we wandered among the huge, high-ceilinged rooms, ogling famous works we'd only seen in tiny reproductions: Monet's *Rouen Cathedral*, Van Gogh's *Cypresses*, Georgia O'Keeffe's *Black Iris*, and Jackson Pollock's *Autumn Rhythm*.

And although I was staring at masterpieces, what I kept seeing was Robinson the night before, shirtless, lying next to me. It made it hard to concentrate. Sometimes, when he looked at me in a certain way, I wondered if he was having the same experience. "A pretty girl who naked is / is worth a million statues." The poet e. e. cummings wrote that. (Not that I'd been totally naked. Just…partially.)

Robinson stopped in front of *Madame X*, a portrait of a beautiful woman by John Singer Sargent, and shook his head in wonder. "We sure don't have art like this in Klamath Falls," he said.

"We don't even have *falls* in Klamath Falls," I replied.

I'd thought that maybe a part of me would miss my hometown. Crappy as it was, it was still mine. But I missed nothing—because everything that truly mattered to me was either already gone or right here next to me in the museum, holding my hand.

When we ended up in front of the Egyptian tomb—the one where Holden Caulfield almost has a breakdown in *The Catcher in the Rye*—Robinson bent to wipe a scuff from the toe of his boot.

"I'll try not to take this as a sign," he said.

"A sign of what?" I asked sharply.

"Doom," Robinson answered. "Isn't stumbling across a pharaoh's tomb worse than, like, a black cat crossing your path? You know, King Tut's curse and all those stories…"

I slid my hand into the back pocket of his jeans. "No, Scalawag, don't be silly. We were randomly walking. We could have just as easily ended up in the café or something."

"Which reminds me—"

"—that you're hungry."

"Exactly." He stood up a little straighter, and I could see the way he shook off his moment of worry. "Do you know what else I want?"

"No," I said, but the word caught in my throat, because I did know, of course. I just wanted to make him show me the answer.

Robinson backed me up against the wall and pressed his lips to mine. My arms circled his waist and I arched myself against him. This was what *I* was hungry for…

A group of kids in Camp Treetop T-shirts filed into the room, so we ducked into the tomb to make out in secret. We hardly even cared when a few giggling kids spied us and called some of their friends over.

But we pulled apart and, exchanging some giggles ourselves, quickly made our exit.

42

OUR FINAL NEW YORK DESTINATION: Nathan's Famous. It was all the way out on Coney Island—which is not actually an island but is so far away from Manhattan on the lurching, sluggish F train that it felt like an entirely different world.

When we finally got there, the beach was as wide and flat as a parking lot, the waves small and distant. There were a lot of people, and some of them were actually swimming, which no one in Oregon did without a wet suit. The Pacific is *cold*.

Though Robinson seemed drained, we strolled along the boardwalk past bumper cars and an arcade popping with digital gunfire. People were flying kites and skateboarding and jogging and hawking cheap souvenirs, like huge foam sunglasses and T-shirts that said KEEP CONEY ISLAND FREAKY.

"You want to ride the Cyclone?" I asked, pointing to the roller coaster in the distance. "Or the Wonder Wheel?"

Robinson shook his head. "Let's just get the hot dogs."

Because he seemed so tired all of a sudden, I suggested, ever so delicately, the idea of going back to the hostel. But Robinson wouldn't hear of it.

"I need my daily dose of nitrates," he said. "Plus, we're tourists, and it's our job to be touristy."

So we turned up Surf Avenue, where the enormous green sign for Nathan's loomed above the street. There was a big outdoor seating area, with seagulls perched near the plastic tables waiting for scraps. The air smelled like the sea and beer and grease. Not that appetizing, in my opinion, but Robinson's whole demeanor had changed. He looked like a kid on Christmas morning.

"How many should I get?" he asked.

"I don't know," I said, scanning the menu. "Two?" I was going to have to order the Caesar salad, since this wasn't exactly the place to get a tofu dog.

Robinson scoffed at two. "Sonya 'the Black Widow' Thomas ate more than forty. Says right there on the sign."

"But that was a hot dog–eating *contest*," I said. "This is just a meal."

Robinson considered the statement. "True. I'll settle for… four. One with chili, one with sauerkraut, and two plain."

"You're taking your life in your hands," I said disapprovingly.

"Only my gastrointestinal tract," Robinson countered, and I grimaced.

Instead of eating with the rest of the crowd, we took our food back to the beach and sat on the warm, gritty sand. It was littered with cigarette butts and half-buried beer cans. But still! The ocean was a gorgeous blue-green, and the weather was perfect, and we were together.

"Can you believe that two weeks ago we were on a beach in California?" Robinson asked.

"Crazy," I said, taking a stab at a limp piece of lettuce. "We've done so much."

Robinson waggled his eyebrows at me. "Not enough, if you know what I mean."

"Pervert," I said, nudging him with my bare toe.

He bit into his second—or was it third?—hot dog and nudged me back.

I decided to abandon my wilted, greasy salad and lay back in the sand, watching the kites swoop and dive above me. I must have fallen asleep for a little while, because when I woke, Robinson wasn't next to me anymore.

CONEY ISLAND

I looked around for a moment, and when I didn't see him, I got up and began walking toward the boardwalk. Maybe he'd gone off to find the Headless Woman or Insectavora, the tattooed fire-eater. Maybe he was buying me a Coney Island shot glass to go with my Cedar Point snow globe.

But he wasn't doing either of those things. Instead, I found him leaning against a fence, shaking.

And vomiting.

I reached out to touch his shoulder, but he waved me away. I took a step back. "You need to see a doctor, Robinson," I pleaded.

After a moment he looked up, his face pale and his eyes red and watering. "Before you go all drama on me," he said, "it was the hot dogs. Not the you-know-what."

"And how do you know that?" I asked.

"I'm *fine* now. And actually, this is totally awesome," he said, wiping his face and trying to smile at me. "I could so beat that Black Widow lady—I'll just eat and barf, eat and barf, and that way I can consume an unlimited number of hot dogs."

I sighed. "You are sick, Robinson. In a lot of ways."

"But you love me," he said, reaching for my hands.

"I do," I said. *So much.*

Robinson fell asleep on the train home, and I practically had to carry him up to our cell in the hostel. He seemed feverish, but I told myself it was just sunburn. Windburn. Whatever it needed to be, as long as it wasn't another infection.

I sat for a long time, listening to the sounds of the city all around us, but mostly just watching him sleep. Were his cheeks less full? His eyes deeper, more sunken? It could be happening so slowly, so subtly, that I hadn't been able to see it…

I lay down beside Robinson and curled my body around his, remembering how I'd refused to tell him a bedtime story back in Las Vegas. I pressed my cheek against his beating heart and vowed I would never say no to him again.

43

"WE HAVE GO TO PHILLY," ROBINSON announced.

"We do?"

He nodded. "I'm not saying this trip is a bucket list or anything, but it is extremely important that I eat a Philly cheesesteak."

I handed our room key to the stoned front-desk clerk, and we stepped into the sunshine. "Tell me you're joking," I said, thinking, *He can't keep a hot dog down, so why on earth is he talking about cheesesteaks?*

Robinson shook his head. "Today I want to do everything, Axi. Every silly thing I can think of."

I put my hand on his waist, slipped my fingers under the edge of his shirt to feel his skin. I could feel him shiver at my touch. "As opposed to yesterday, or the day before, when you were a good boy and did only what others told you to do?"

He laughed and wrapped his arms around me. "Okay, you have a point."

I didn't want to spoil the mood, but I had to say what I was thinking. "We've had a lot of fun, and we can definitely keep on having it. But I think you should see a doctor, just to be sure."

Robinson shook his head again, this time more emphatically. "No can do, Aximoron. Places to go, people to see…"

I looked at him carefully, weighing his stubbornness against mine. If I fought hard now, maybe I could get him to go. Just a minor checkup, I'd say, a quick ear to the lungs and heart, maybe a *tiny* little X-ray and reading of his LDH levels. I'd sit in the waiting room, staring at stale magazines and waiting for good news.

Because maybe it would work out. Who was to say it couldn't?

On the other hand, if Robinson went to the hospital, he would resent me for it. Intensely, and possibly eternally.

Whose trip is it, Axi? I asked myself. *Yours? Or his?* Because in the end, someone had to make the call.

"It's less than two hours away," Robinson said, interrupting my thoughts. "It's not like I'm asking you to drive me to Daytona."

"You're not going to do that next, are you?"

"No, ma'am. Scout's honor."

I sighed. "Fine," I said. "You win."

He smiled his beautiful smile. "I love it when you roll your eyes like that," he said. "It's adorable."

"Oh, stop."

"And when you sort of wrinkle up your nose, like you smell something funny, but it's really that you're trying to decide whether to laugh or be annoyed."

"Oh, *really*. What else do you love about me?" I was annoyed, but it was at myself rather than at Robinson. Or not annoyed, exactly—more like...scared.

We were at the car now, and I was climbing into the driver's seat. "Let's hear it," I said. I pulled into the street and pointed us toward the Holland Tunnel. You'd almost think I had a license to drive.

"Well, everything," Robinson said. "But specifically? The list is kind of long."

"You are such a flatterer," I said.

Robinson didn't say anything for a while after that. In fact, we were on the other side of the river before he spoke, and I thought he'd fallen asleep.

"I love how you touch the tip of your nose when you're thinking hard about something," he said, turning to fix his gaze on me. "I love how you tuck your hair behind your ears but it always slips right back down immediately. I love your eyes and your perfect lips. I love that your nail polish, when you bother to wear it, is always chipped. I love how you use fancy words that I have to look up at home. I love the tiny little crescent moon of a birthmark on the tip of your left pinkie. I love the way—"

I didn't need to hear any more. I needed to kiss him. So I pulled over to the side of the road, and there, with the New York City skyline behind us, I did.

"It's going to take a lot longer to get to Philly this way," Robinson said, talking and kissing and smiling all at once.

"We have time," I said. "We have so much time."

44

"SO, SCALAWAG, DO YOU WANT TO GO TO Pat's King of Steaks or Geno's?" I asked, poking Robinson awake—gently, of course. We'd made it to Philly in under two hours, and now I was parked between the two cheesesteak institutions, which stood a block away from each other like captains of opposing teams.

Robinson yawned and stretched. "You know," he said, frowning slightly, "I'm not actually that hungry right now." For a moment he placed his hand over his stomach—a strange kind of gesture for him. "What I'd like is a nice warm drink."

I looked at him sharply. It was eighty degrees out, and I was sweating against the truck seat. "You're not cold, are you?"

Being cold meant that Robinson might have a fever, and if he had a fever, that meant he might have an infection, and if he had an infection, then he needed to get to a hospital. Stat. Because infections in what doctors like to call an immunocompromised person—a person like Robinson, who'd had high-dose chemo, radiation therapy, and a stem cell transplant—could be deadly.

I reached toward his forehead to feel it, but he brushed my hand away. "No!" he said, a little too loudly. "I just thought some tea sounded nice. Then we go get the cheesesteak."

He got out of the truck and started walking. I stayed where I was, staring at him through the windshield, feeling both mad and worried. What was I supposed to do? Drag him to the ER so they could take his temperature? He wouldn't let me.

I got out and caught up to him—easily, because he was walking at an old man's pace. Like every step took concentration and effort.

"A little caffeine and I'll be good to go," he said, pointing to a coffee shop at the end of the block.

Please be right about that, I thought. I took his hand.

In the café we found a window table and sank into the worn but comfortable seats. Then a salesman type burst in and commandeered the table next to us, talking on his cell phone and at the same time waving the waitress over, as if it were a matter of life and death that he got served before we did. "...QR codes are going to increase the conversion rate of your sales funnel—" he was saying. When the waitress walked by he shouted, "Large Earl Grey with soy milk on the side and raw sugar, *two lumps*."

Robinson glared at him for a moment. "This is the City of Brotherly Love, jerk," he muttered. Then he rested his head on the table. "Man. I don't know why I'm so tired."

I wanted to scream, *Because you have cancer?*

Instead, I reached out and ran my fingers through his thick, dark hair. I'd almost forgotten what he looked like without it. It took a while to grow back after the chemo, but when it did, he grew it longer.

"That feels good," he said, his voice muffled.

I took a deep breath, steeling myself for what I had to say.

"Robinson, we need to get you back to a hospital—actually, *our* hospital. I'll use my credit card and we'll fly home. We can be there in ten hours."

"I don't like planes," Robinson said to the tabletop.

"You have to see Dr. Suzuki. Now. She'll know what to do."

"Every time I hear her name, I think about violin lessons. Have you heard of the Suzuki method of teaching music?"

"*Don't* change the subject."

Robinson lifted his head from the table. His tired eyes met mine. "You say she'll know what to do. But what if there's nothing to be done?"

"There's always something to be done," I said, my voice rising. I didn't like this new fatalistic tone of his at all.

"You've planned everything so perfectly, Axi. Please don't get all freaked out now."

I reached for his hands and gripped them hard. "But when does it end, Robinson? We can't run like this forever."

"We're not going to," he assured me. "We just have one more stop to make. It's the last one."

"One last stop?" I asked. "Where's that? Please don't say you want to go to New Orleans to eat jambalaya or something."

He laughed and squeezed my fingers. "No. My stomach is no longer dictating our travels. But it's...well, it's a couple of states away."

"A couple of *states*?" I repeated. I doubted Chuck the Truck would make it that far.

247

Next to us the salesman had begun shouting. "No, Ed, the goal is to *shorten* the amount of time it takes the *probable purchaser* to become a *product owner*!"

Both Robinson and I glared at him now. He'd taken a table that could have seated six, and he was treating it like his desk. Scattered across it were his iPad, a BlackBerry, a leather binder, a copy of the *Philadelphia Inquirer*, car keys…

His car keys.

It was then that I had an idea that would have shocked the old Axi Moore to the depths of her soul. Good thing she no longer existed.

"Axi?" Robinson said, waving a hand in front of my face. "Aren't you going to get on my case for not telling you where I want to go?"

"Yes," I said distractedly. "Later." I was staring at the salesman. *Get up*, I thought. *Get up.*

"The numbers don't add up, Ed," he yelled.

And then, as if what I'd just imagined was totally meant to be, the salesman stood. Still yammering into his Bluetooth, he made his way toward the bathrooms.

I got up and threw a five on the table. "Meet me at the southeast corner of the block," I said, and I was out the door before Robinson had even opened his mouth to ask me why.

Outside, I half-jogged down the street, clicking the automatic lock button on the key chain and watching for the answering flicker of headlights. Would it be the blue Acura? The silver Toyota? I had such a mighty sense of purpose that

I hardly noticed the racing of my heart. I was taking care of Robinson. If he needed to go somewhere, I was going to see to it that his journey took place in a reliable vehicle.

I'd crossed onto the next block and was nearing the third without a single chirp of a car. My pulse quickened and my head began to hurt.

I was stealing a car.

In broad daylight.

Fear began to trump my sense of purpose. I started jogging faster. *Where are you? Flash your lights*, I whispered, like I had magical powers or something. Or phenomenal luck. It didn't matter which.

Finally, when I was about to give up, I heard the beep of a horn answering its remote key. I turned toward the sound and gasped. It was a midnight-blue Mustang GT. A convertible.

I started cackling like a crazy person. Robinson was going to freak out.

Easy as pie, I opened the driver's-side door and jumped in. The seats were tan leather, and the inside sparkled like that salesman spit-shined it every morning. He was going to seriously miss his ride. A wave of remorse came over me, but I shook it off.

The Mustang practically leapt into the street. I pulled up to our truck and quickly tossed our bags in at the same time I called to Robinson, who was leaning against a telephone pole as if standing up on his own was too much work. "Hurry, the bus is leaving."

He walked toward me and his eyes widened. "Wha—"

"Just get in."

It took him another second to wrap his head around the directive. But then he slid in next to me, and I gunned the engine.

And we were gone.

"How—what—I don't—" Robinson stuttered. "Am I—"

"Keys, Clyde," I said, feigning complete nonchalance. "They're *so* much easier than a cordless drill."

"I just don't—" He couldn't even finish a sentence.

"I borrowed them from the loud guy in the coffee shop."

Robinson's eyes widened even further as he looked around the car. He ran his hand over the dashboard. "Four-point-six-liter V-8 with three-fifteen horsepower and three hundred twenty-five pound-feet of torque. Pure American-made muscle. This thing is a beast, Axi." He turned to beam at me. "Just when I thought I could not possibly love you more."

He began to laugh—a strong laugh like I hadn't heard in days. "Seriously, *thank God*," he finally said, gasping for breath. "For a minute, I really, truly thought I'd died and gone to heaven."

45

ROBINSON TOLD ME TO DRIVE SOUTH, so I did. For once, no questions asked. I'd do anything he asked me, and I had to admit, the Mustang was a major step up from the truck. It had power steering, air-conditioning, and, according to Robinson, "an aftermarket Bose speaker system that costs more than a new Kia." It just ate up the miles.

He was staring sleepily out the window now, watching the world go by the way I used to do. "Have you noticed," he said once, "how this entire country is, like, in patterns? It goes city, then suburban sprawl, then farmland. And then city, suburban sprawl, farmland again..."

"And you're never more than fifty miles from a McDonald's," I joked.

"That's a relief," he answered.

Later that evening, after speeding through Delaware, Maryland, and half of Virginia, I pulled into a rest stop in the middle of the Blue Ridge Mountains. In the humid twilight, I spread out our sleeping bags near the border of trees. I didn't bother with the tent, because I didn't want to draw any attention our way. According to the strange logic of the interstate rest area system, *sleeping* is fine, but camping isn't. And although camping at a rest area would be pretty low on my list of crimes and misdemeanors, I saw no reason to be awakened by a cop tapping his flashlight on our tent pole.

I held out the Slim Jim I'd bought for Robinson at the last gas station, but he shook his head. "That Filet-O-Fish we had for dinner is sitting in my stomach like a ball of lead," he groaned. "I think I'm going to have to sleep it off."

"I told you to order the salad," I said. "It was good."

He snorted. "Getting a salad at McDonald's is like going into Car Toys and coming out with a pencil sharpener." He slipped into the sleeping bag, not bothering to remove anything but the belt from his jeans.

"Well, I feel just fine," I said a bit huffily.

"Well, *you* don't have cancer," he snapped.

I sucked in my breath sharply and held it. In the silence that followed, I heard the crickets chirping and the rushing waves of cars passing by on the highway. If I closed my eyes, I could almost imagine it was the sound of the ocean.

I felt Robinson reaching for my hand. "I'm sorry," he whispered. "I shouldn't have said that."

I turned to him, tears now wetting my cheeks. "What, we should just pretend that everything's all right? We should just believe what we want to believe? Is that what we should do, Robinson?"

He was quiet for a moment, his brow furrowed in concentration. "I don't know what we should do," he said softly. "Wake up and drive some more tomorrow. Try to laugh. Love each other. I mean, what else is there?"

"I'm scared," I whispered.

"There's nothing to be afraid of, Axi." He brought my hand up to his lips and kissed it, right in the center of my palm.

"Again, is that what we *want* to believe? I just feel like we're stumbling forward now, hoping for the best. I mean, where are we going? And where is the road map? The metaphorical one, I mean—the directions. LEGO sets come with directions. Temporary tattoos come with directions. Once I saw an entire Web page dedicated to telling you how to order coffee from Starbucks!"

"Really?"

"Yes! Step one is 'Decide what you want to order before your turn in line.' I'm like, oh, really? Wow! Thank you so much! I never would have thought of that."

Robinson was laughing now. I was glad I'd cheered him up, but I wasn't feeling any better. "Where are the directions for the big things? Because I want them," I cried. "What are the instructions for, I don't know, *life?*"

Robinson's laugh slowly faded. "Axi, if we had directions, it wouldn't be life. It would be an assignment. Grunt work. Not knowing is a major part of the deal."

I knew he was right, but I didn't like it. Sighing, I scooted as close to him as possible, but the zippers of our sleeping bags kept us apart.

"'As far as the laws of mathematics refer to reality, they are not certain; and as far as they are certain, they do not refer to reality,'" I said.

"Huh?" said Robinson.

"Einstein," I said. "Mr. Fox had that written at the top of his chalkboard."

"I like it," Robinson said.

"Well, I want certainty," I said.

I felt like Robinson and I were caught between two different worlds. There was the world we'd been living in—a world of freedom, beauty, and, *okay*, yes, utterly wonderful and terrible irresponsibility—and then there was the darker, sadder world that I sensed we were about to enter. I wanted to know how to navigate it.

Robinson tilted his head closer to mine. "You can put it on your Christmas list."

I turned away. "Don't patronize me. I don't even know where we're driving to."

Robinson rolled over and stared up at the sky. It was a deep, velvety blue, and little pinpricks of stars were appearing, more and more every minute. "Here is certainty," he said. "I love you, Axi Moore. And I will never not love you, for the rest of my life."

The tears came again, and I didn't bother to wipe them away. "I love you, too," I whispered. "For the rest of my life."

We kissed, wrapping our arms around each other and holding on tight. And then, exhausted, we said good night and closed our eyes to sleep.

Lying there in the summer night, it was almost as if I could feel the earth moving beneath us, turning on its axis. And as I listened to the crickets singing to each other, I wondered if the rest of my life and the rest of Robinson's life meant two entirely different lengths of time.

How do you know anything for sure? I thought. But I knew the answer to that already. *You don't.*

Finally I fell asleep. In the middle of the night, Robinson and I rolled toward each other, our arms crossing. The night seemed to hold us, too, in a big, soft, dark embrace.

Robinson's voice was low and groggy. "Maybe we should get married," he said.

I couldn't speak; my heart was too full. Full of joy and surprise—and futility, too, because they don't let you do that at sixteen. I put my head on his chest, wishing I could melt into him entirely. The best I could do was match my breathing to his long, steady breaths. In a moment, I realized that he was asleep again.

It was possible he hadn't even been truly awake in the first place.

46

IN THE EARLY AFTERNOON, SOMEWHERE in North Carolina, we took an exit off the highway and ended up in a park, near the shore of a small lake.

"Let's stop for a little while," Robinson said. "I like this spot."

Ringed by trees and rolling hills, the lake was calm, reflecting the blue sky back at itself. I rolled down the window and breathed in the smell of clean, piney air. "It's pretty here," I agreed.

We climbed out of the Mustang and walked toward the edge of the shimmering water. Robinson bent down, selected a flat stone, and then skipped it across the surface—one, two, three times.

He snorted. "Terrible. I used to be able to do twelve."

I stood beside him and snaked my arm around his waist. It felt so good to be off the road—to feel my muscles loosening, my gas-pedal foot slowly uncramping. "Maybe we should rent a paddleboat or something. Take a break. Drive some more later."

It was like he hadn't even heard me. "I used to love coming here," he said.

"What?"

His eyes swept over the lake, but he seemed to be seeing some other thing. Or some other time. "We used to build these crazy rafts and tow them over in wagons. Then we'd see how many kids we could pile on them before they'd sink. We'd get in trouble because you need a permit for a boat. And we'd

always argue that we weren't on a boat—we were on a raft made by nine-year-olds out of packing crates and big pieces of Styrofoam."

"Wait a second," I said, dropping my arm from his waist and taking a step back. "Are you talking about *this* lake?"

"Of course," Robinson said. "I was born three miles away."

Before I could stop myself, I shoved him, and he stumbled a little. "I'm so sorry," I said, grabbing his hand. "But wait. You brought me…home?"

"I wanted you to meet my parents," Robinson said, as if this were the simplest, least surprising thing in the world.

I was totally gobsmacked. I didn't even know where we were, really, and now I was about to meet Robinson's parents, who until now had been about as real to me as a couple of unicorns.

"Welcome to Asheville, North Carolina," Robinson said, gesturing to the trees and paths and joggers around us. "Formerly Tuberculosis Central, and now known as the Paris of the South, or, to the writers of *Rolling Stone*, the New Freak Capital of the US."

I shook my head in disbelief. I didn't know whether to kiss him or kick him. "You wait until now to tell me?"

He smiled. "A guy ought to surprise his girl once in a while," he said. "It's romantic that way. Now let's go see the sights, such as they are."

And for the next hour, he showed me around his hometown. I saw the shop where he bought his first guitar; the elm tree

that he broke his arm falling out of; the elementary school where he'd started a rock 'n' roll club. ("It got huge, even though some super-ancient dudes protested, saying rock 'n' roll was 'the devil's music,'" Robinson said proudly.)

Nothing was particularly special—and yet everything was extraordinary because it was a part of Robinson's previously classified childhood. I wanted to stop at every corner, peer in every window. I wanted to stop strangers and ask them to tell me a story about Robinson. He'd opened the door to his past, and I wanted to walk right through it.

Robinson touched my arm, directing my attention toward a drugstore sandwiched between a café and a crystal shop. "Look," he said. "There's even a place like Ernie's. But the coffee's even worse—it's like battery acid. I swear it once ate a hole in my jeans." He shook his head at the memory. "Of course, it could have been actual battery acid that did that. I certainly spent enough time in my dad's shop."

"His shop?" I asked.

"He owns a car repair shop. Robinson's Repairs."

"Wow, he named it after you?"

Robinson shrugged noncommittally. "Sort of."

"What do you mean, sort of? Who else would it be—the Swiss Family Robinson? Jackie Robinson? Robinson Crusoe? Smokey Rob—"

"Hey, see that?" he interrupted. "That's the streetlight that my brother ran his custom-built Cheemer into."

"Cheemer?" I said. "I don't know what a Cheemer is." Clearly the shop-naming conversation wasn't going anywhere.

"A Chevrolet with a BMW engine," Robinson explained. "You know, Chevy plus Beemer? Jay Leno has one."

"Oh," I said, wishing these names meant anything to me. "So it's like an automotive mash-up."

He laughed. "Exactly. It's the car version of that Eazy-E and Johnny Cash thing, 'Folsom Prison Gangstaz.' *I got beat for the street, Ta pump in ya jeep—*"

"You should probably stop," I said. "That guy over there is looking at you funny."

"Like I care," Robinson replied, but he stopped anyway. He seemed tired again. "Drive that way, why don't you?" He pointed vaguely to the east, and that was how I saw the Biltmore House, an enormous Gilded Age chateau built by a Vanderbilt whose name Robinson couldn't recall. It looked like a fairy-tale castle—a place where Cinderella would live happily ever after with her prince.

Where was my happily-ever-after, I wanted to know. Why did that silly girl get one when my chances were so slim?

Without even thinking, I pulled onto the shoulder of the road. I looked over at Robinson as if I were about to ask him those questions.

"Oh, this is perfect," he said. "This is a very special place."

I looked around. We were stopped in the middle of a bunch of trees. "What's so great about it?"

Robinson unbuckled my seat belt and pulled me toward him. He brought his mouth close to mine and whispered, "It's where I did *this*."

And then he kissed me, so long and sweet and tender that I almost cried—because here we were, together, and maybe this was finally the end of the road.

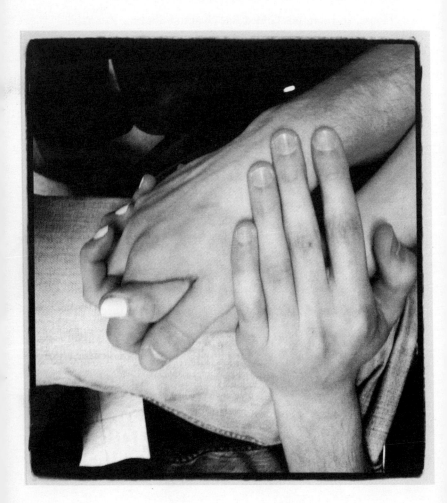

47

THE HOUSE WAS A THREE-STORY
Victorian with a high, round turret, stained-glass windows, and an enormous porch. The front steps bowed in the middle, and the paint was beginning to fade and peel. But it was picturesque that way—a little bit of shabby chic.

There were rosebushes everywhere, blossoming in all different colors: snow-white, yellow tipped with sunset orange, the soft pink of a ballet slipper. The roses climbed a trellis on the porch and spilled over the railings, filling the air with their glorious perfume.

I climbed the steps after Robinson, cold with nerves. He gave me a quick squeeze and then rang the doorbell.

For a moment, nothing happened. I heard a voice and barking inside, and then a woman who I assumed was Robinson's mother appeared in the doorway. When she saw who had rung, she opened her mouth as if to shout, but instead she fell to the floor—she just sort of crumpled in the hall, like a marionette whose strings had been cut.

Robinson yelped, "Mom!" And he went to help her up, but before he got to her, a man who had to be Robinson's dad appeared in the hall. He saw Robinson, and for a second he just gaped at him.

They were acting like they'd seen a ghost.

Awkward! I thought—and they had yet to even notice me, the other unannounced visitor.

Of course, if I showed up at my apartment after vanishing the way I had, my dad would probably assume I was some booze-induced hallucination and slam the door in my face.

Robinson's dad slowly bent down to pick up his wife. It was like they were in some kind of slow motion. When they both were finally vertical again, their shock started giving way to a kind of joy I couldn't remember seeing in my father since I was a little girl. Robinson's mom grabbed her son and squeezed him *hard*. "Oh my God!" she cried. "You're here! I missed you so much!"

Robinson's dad was wiping his eyes, trying to keep it together. He reached out and grasped Robinson's shoulder. "Oscar," he said, his voice full of wonder and relief, "you came back."

Robinson was blinking hard and fast and maybe sniffling a little bit. And I was crying, too, at the sight of their reunion, and at the same time thinking, *Oscar? Who's Oscar?*

The barking began again, and a small brown dog came waddling up as fast as her short legs would carry her. "Leafy!" Robinson cried.

She was as fat as a sausage, and her whole body wagged while her tail stayed still. Robinson got down on the floor, and she proceeded to attack him in an ecstasy of yipping and licking. "Sit, girl," he said, laughing, and she obeyed him for about five milliseconds before launching herself at him again. "I love you, too," he said, rubbing her long brown ears.

Then a tall man who looked almost exactly like an older, burlier Robinson came into the hallway and said, "What's all the ruckus?"

When he saw Robinson, he rushed forward. He looked like he was going to tackle Robinson, and without thinking I jumped in and shot my arm out, as if I—all five feet five inches and 120 pounds of me—could block his charge.

The man stopped short and said, "Wow, hot bodyguard, man."

I flushed as Robinson and his brother hugged and slapped each other on the back.

Then Robinson stepped away and put his arm protectively around my shoulders. "Everyone," he said, "this is Axi." He looked down at me and smiled. "My partner in crime." And then in front of everyone, he kissed me—a little less chastely than I might have expected.

"Well, well," said his mother, sniffling and trying to smile at me, too. "Axi, I'm glad to meet you." And then instead of shaking my hand, she pulled me close into her rose-smelling neck, and I realized how long it had been since a mother—any mother—had held me. "Oh, I'm sorry, dear," she said, patting the damp spot she'd made on my shirt. She laughed, embarrassed. "I'm a bit overwhelmed."

Robinson made the rest of the introductions. "That's my brother, Jonathan. He's twenty, but he's probably still living here, because he's a bum like that." The affection was obvious in Robinson's voice.

Jonathan pretended to take offense. "I've got my own place," he said. "I'm just over here borrowing Dad's tools."

"And waiting to see what your mother will make for dinner," his father added.

"Maybe," Jonathan allowed.

Robinson said, "And this is my dad, Joe, and my mom, Louise, but everyone calls her Lou."

"And what about you?" I whispered. "Oscar?"

He gave a slightly embarrassed shrug. "You can see why I go by Robinson," he said. Then he pulled me close to him again. "I promise," he whispered, "that's the last of my secrets."

48

AFTER A DELICIOUS DINNER OF LASAGNA, garlic bread, and salad, during which there were more tears and more fits of laughter than I could count, Robinson took my hand and led me to the back of the house.

"I wasn't allowed to have girls in my room," he said, "but I'm going to assume my parents are over that by now." He pushed on a rather rickety door, but instead of opening into a bedroom, it led to a porch, with windows on all three sides. The painted wooden floor was scuffed and pitched; there was a wicker love seat along one wall and a double bed shoved against another. Guitars and amps were arranged in the corners, alongside neat stacks of CDs.

"This is your bedroom?" I asked, thinking of my dark closet of a room back home.

"It's the old sleeping porch. This place was once a boarding-house for TB patients," Robinson said. "People with tuberculosis

exercise the right to think for yourself

were supposed to sleep in fresh air, so there are rooms like this all over Asheville."

"I love it," I said, running my finger along the windowsill.

Robinson sank down onto the bed. "I slept on the floor out here for two weeks," he said. "Staking my claim. Finally, they said it could be mine."

I sat down next to him. The sheets were clean and the pillows freshly plumped; either someone had sneaked in to make the bed, or Robinson's mother had kept up his room as if he'd only gone out for a walk. "Your parents are amazing.

Why weren't you with them—all along?" I asked.

Robinson frowned. "We went to Portland because of the experimental immunotherapy program with Dr. Suzuki. She's the best there is, right? But my parents were living in this terrible motel and going to the hospital every day, and it was just awful. It was too hard on them. I said, 'Please go home. This isn't what I want. I don't want you to see me go through this.'"

"And they just *left*?" I don't know why it shocked me as it did, considering the way my own mother split town.

"They didn't want to, believe me. But I made them. I said if things got really bad, obviously they could come back. But things didn't get really bad—they got better. The immuno-therapy was helping, and I got discharged from the hospital."

"The same day as me," I said, smiling at the memory of that perfect morning.

"Right. And I'd planned to come back here, but then there was the problem of you."

"The *problem*?" I asked.

He smiled. "The problem of having a giant crush on you and you not knowing it," he said. "But conveniently, my uncle had just moved close to your hometown. You were going to K-Falls, and I decided to follow you. I wanted to be with you."

I flushed. "I'm glad you did. But still—I can't believe they let you do it."

"I told them I'd come back here in the fall. Do senior year

at my old school. They understood—I wanted to pretend like I was normal, at a school where no one knew I had cancer. I was just a kid who got to study somewhere else for a while." He smiled. "A semester abroad, in bucolic K-Falls."

I snorted. "You'd better look up *bucolic* in the dictionary."

"I don't have to, because I have you," Robinson said, rolling his eyes.

"Oh, right," I said, nudging him with my foot. But his story still didn't entirely make sense to me. "Why wouldn't you ever talk about your family? Why were they such a huge secret?"

Robinson sighed. "I didn't like talking about them because I felt so guilty. I knew it was selfish of me to be away from them. But I wanted to see things, Axi. I wanted to have a bigger life." He reached up and twisted a strand of my hair around his fingers. "I wanted to fall in love."

I nodded. It wasn't totally insane, I guess. "But you, like, wrote them and stuff?"

"Of course," he said. "They knew I was okay."

"But what about this trip? How'd you explain that?"

He smiled. "I told them school was out—"

"Even though you weren't in school anymore," I interrupted.

"Well, they didn't know that. And they weren't going to check the calendar and see that there were three more weeks of classes I should have been in. I told them I was going to Camp Motorsport. It's a summer camp for gearheads." He paused thoughtfully. "It sounded pretty cool, actually…"

I rolled my eyes. "You're crazy."

"But you love me."

I leaned over and kissed him on the side of his soft mouth. "I do."

A blast of music came from the garage, where Robinson had said Jonathan was fixing up an old Buick into a custom racer.

"Did you know we'd come here, then?" I asked.

Robinson shook his head. "I thought we'd go back to Oregon first. But then…"

He didn't finish the sentence, but I could fill it in. He'd started feeling sick. And he'd wanted to go home.

I understood that. I'd want to run to my mom, too, if I had one who was any use to me. If I knew what *state* she was living in.

I looked out the window then, and I saw all these floating lights. They were yellowish green, flashing on and off. "What are those?" I asked.

Robinson gaped at me. "Haven't you ever seen a firefly before? A lightning bug?"

"A what? No! We don't have them in Oregon."

Robinson sat up and peered out at the lawn. "I had no idea you were so deprived. They're the best bugs in the world because they can light their butts up. It's how they find mates."

"They're beautiful," I said.

Robinson reached up and brushed the hair from my face. "Not like you."

"Don't be corny."

"I'm not. I'm dead serious." He paused. "Dying serious, I should say."

"No, you should *not* say that."

Robinson sighed. "Oh, Axi, I'm tired," he said. "Tell me a bedtime story."

"Sing me a bedtime lullaby," I said with a smile. "Like in Vegas." I had every intention of giving in this time, but not that easily.

"Story," he insisted.

"Song."

"I'll flip a coin," he said.

"No! Don't!" I yelped.

He looked at me strangely. "Why not?"

"Just don't."

"Okay, fine. Then you have to tell the story."

We lay back on the bed. I took a deep breath and began. A fairy-tale beginning. "Once upon a time, there was a girl and a boy."

"So far so good," Robinson said. He rolled over so that his face was in my neck. "The girl was always bossing the boy around," he said, his lips brushing my skin. "She kept telling him to eat better."

"The girl had only the boy's best interests at heart," I retorted.

"Mmmm," said Robinson. Already his voice was thick with sleep.

"She wanted to take care of him," I whispered. "And to be taken care of by him."

I paused, listening to the music coming from the garage. It was Bob Dylan, I thought, but I didn't know the song.

"She knew how lucky they were," I went on, "because they had found each other. She understood that sometimes people had to search for years to find what they wanted. Whereas some—the charmed few—just stumble upon it. Like children on a beach. Some come home with only rocks and broken shells, while others unearth a perfect sand dollar, fragile but beautiful."

Robinson sighed. By now he was sleeping.

"And the girl understood something else—and maybe the boy did, too. Love was magical and infinite. But luck, in the end, was not."

Out in the garage, Jonathan turned up the music, and Dylan's nasal, sandpapery voice finally reached me clearly. *"The future for me is already a thing of the past. You were my first love and you will be my last."*

I clenched my fists against my sides. I looked out the window for a star to wish on, but clouds had come in the evening. The only lights were those of the fireflies, turning on and off, on and off.

49

ROBINSON'S PARENTS WELCOMED ME like a family member—and they said nothing about me spending the night in their son's room. Joe, who was a history buff, told me all about the Asheville tuberculosis sanitariums the next morning. (Even F. Scott Fitzgerald, my ninth-grade literary crush, had spent time in one.) Jonathan walked me around the car he was working on, explaining various things about its engine that I didn't understand and promising to take me for a ride as soon as he got new tires. Lou bought tempeh bacon when Robinson mentioned I didn't eat meat, and one afternoon she braided my hair.

"I always wanted a daughter," she said wistfully. "Those boys and their cars. I love them to the moon, but it's horsepower this and carburetor that, and I always thought to myself, *Who's going to help me prune the roses?*"

"I don't have much experience with gardening," I admitted. Dad and I had had a spider plant in our apartment, but it was probably all dried up by then.

"You'd like it," Lou said. "You're a careful person, I can see that."

Used to be, anyway, I thought.

"It's like the Little Prince says," she went on. "'You become responsible, forever, for what you have tamed. You are responsible for your rose.' You can't tame a stock car, Axi. It's not the same thing."

I smiled. "I've quoted that book to your son."

"Oscar—I mean Robinson, I guess—could never be persuaded to read it."

And then we walked outside, into the soft summer air, and she showed me how to deadhead the roses so they'd bloom all the way until late fall. When we came back, we had armfuls of blossoms, enough to put in every room.

The point is, life with Robinson's family would have been perfect if only Robinson hadn't been getting sicker, minute by minute. It was as if being back home allowed him to finally stop pretending he was all right. And had there been any doubt about his prognosis—or any denial of what it meant—a visit from his childhood specialist had wiped that away.

"I recommend you call hospice," the doctor had said. Meaning: all you can do now is keep him comfortable. *Until.*

Word spread quickly around town, and visitors began to arrive, bringing casseroles and cookies and boxes of Kleenex. There was a procession of friends, neighbors, classmates, and soccer coaches who had known and loved Robinson.

Robinson held court on the old sofa in the living room, pale and covered with blankets, even though the rest of us were in short sleeves and dabbing at our sweating upper lips. His spirits were high, though he tired easily. And though he was in pain, he rarely hit the button on his morphine IV—he said it made his head feel like a hot-air balloon.

Everyone had stories to tell, like the time Robinson won the Soap Box Derby race, then just kept going for another half mile because he'd neglected to give his car a set of brakes. About how he'd "borrowed" the high school's mascot costume to perform a gut-busting bump-and-grind during halftime at the homecoming game. One neighbor told me that Robinson mowed and raked her lawn for her but always refused payment, and a pimply twelve-year-old told me that when he was eight, Robinson had saved him from drowning in Beaver Lake.

It was as if I was seeing Robinson's life flash before my eyes, in the words and stories of the people who loved him.

When he felt good enough, Robinson entertained his guests with tales of life "out West," which he made sound way better than it actually was.

"If Klamath Falls has a boom in tourism, it'll be because of you," I told him one evening. "And they'll all come home disappointed."

"K-Falls has its charms," he said.

"Oh yeah? Name one."

"Her name is Axi Moore," he said. "Sheesh, that was easy. Oh, and Wubba's BBQ Express has that great pulled pork sandwich."

See what I mean? Spirits high.

During the days, I passed around snacks and reheated bowls of pasta or soup in the microwave. Even though we in the house weren't hungry, everyone else was. It was like a dinner party that never ended.

Lou moved through the house as if in a dream, or a nightmare. Joe looked pale and scared. Jonathan, on Robinson's orders, hung a sign on the wall that said NO CRYING ALLOWED— not that anyone was capable of following that particular order.

Even fat Leafy whined and barked, as if she had stories about Robinson, too.

"She used to be an agility champ," Joe said once, shaking his head. "Can you believe it?"

"Now she's an eating champ," Jonathan added, tossing her a cracker.

I bent down and rubbed Leafy's feathery ears, and she responded with a warm lick of my hand. I had a sudden pang of longing for my old dog. Or maybe it was a longing for the healthy, loving family I'd never really had. It was hard to tell.

50

"CLOSE YOUR EYES," ROBINSON SAID. He was reaching into the drawer by the side of his bed. I pretended to squint, then opened my eyes wide as he pulled out a pocketknife with a gleaming silver blade.

"When a knife's around, I like to pay attention," I said. "Sort of as a matter of policy."

He laughed, then coughed. "I'm not going to point it at you," he said. "Only this." He gestured toward the sleeping porch's wainscoting.

"What are you going to do?"

"It's a surprise," he said. "You'll see. Just close your eyes."

I watched him dig the tip into the wood, and then I did as he asked. I don't know how much time passed, but I must have fallen asleep, because the next thing I knew, Robinson was nudging me awake. "Look," he said.

Carved into the wall of the porch was a message: B&C4EVER.

"Bonnie and Clyde," he said. He was smiling at me, his perfect, crooked grin. "That's us."

"Forever," I said.

We lay back down, and Robinson wrapped his arms around me. I traced the veins of his wrist, their delicate blue lines showing through his skin like a road map, and I thought of the map in my backpack, the one we'd marked with every stop: LA. The redwoods. Detroit. I thought, too, of my bag of souvenirs. Magical objects—a snow globe, a glass orb—that in certain lights looked exactly like junk.

"I miss you already," Robinson said softly.

"I'm here," I whispered back. "I'll always be here."

"But I won't," he said.

In my chest swelled an ache unfathomably deep and dark. And I said nothing, because I knew he was right. I kissed his face, his lips—and then somehow, we slept.

But in the middle of the night, we woke up, and without words we turned toward each other. Robinson's hands reached for me, and his mouth pressed itself against my neck. I brought his face up to mine, hungry to taste his lips. We kissed, and I heard a low moan—mine. I realized I was trembling.

Robinson smiled, lightly tracing the lines of my brow, my nose, my mouth. "Don't be nervous," he whispered.

How could I not be nervous? I knew what was going to happen. The air was charged with it. We were going to kiss until we were breathless, and then...and *then*...

I moved closer to him, running my hand along his hip and down his thigh. I felt him shiver as I brushed my fingers along the smoothness of his stomach.

He caught my hand and held it. "I love you," he said.

"I love you back," I whispered. And then I slid my fingers out of his so I could touch him again.

We kissed for what seemed like hours—sometimes tenderly, sometimes almost desperately. Sometimes we stopped and just looked at each other. As if we were memorizing our bodies and memorizing this moment. I felt like I was made of nothing but longing.

Then Robinson pulled away, and I watched as he slipped his shirt over his head. His white skin seemed to glow in the half-light. He looked at me questioningly, and then he reached for the buttons on my blouse. He was whispering my name.

"Do you want to—" he asked.

"*Yes*," I said.

We wriggled out of the rest of our clothes, and then I wrapped my arms around his back. I guided him toward me. I wanted to pull him into my body—as if we could become one person; as if, finally, I could protect him.

Robinson was breathing hard and we were kissing. I touched him everywhere, even as I felt myself dissolving. He was whispering words into my mouth, but I couldn't concentrate on what they were, because something inside me was unfurling. I was no longer Axi Moore. I was me and I was him; I was the night and the stars. The two of us lay on that bed and shuddered with desire.

Afterward, he slept right against me, and I stared at our initials in the flickering candlelight. B&C4EVER.

And somehow I knew it was true. We would be together forever.

51

I OPENED MY EYES TO THE SOUND OF BIRDS making a loud and unmelodious racket in the big oaks in the backyard. I snuggled closer to Robinson, glad they hadn't woken him up, too. Leafy, who'd taken to standing guard outside his room at night, came in when she heard the rustling of blankets, and sat at the foot of the bed. She immediately began whining, because she knew I couldn't resist those big brown eyes of hers. In the four days we'd been here, I'd already fed her almost an entire box of treats.

"Hush, Leafy," I said. "Be patient."

She wagged her tail and whined more loudly, and when I didn't immediately go in search of the Milk-Bones, she began to bark.

"Quiet," I whispered. "Robinson's asleep."

But behind me there was no movement, despite the noise, and a terrible, panicky feeling came over me. I turned to look at Robinson's chest, and I saw that it wasn't rising or falling. *He wasn't breathing.* And suddenly I was backing out of the bed, my hands clutched to my face.

Leafy began yapping even more loudly—a treat was coming any minute now, she was sure of it—and I didn't bother to shush her because it didn't matter. *Nothing* mattered. I dug my nails into my cheeks, and the tears came out fast and hot. I was gasping for breath, and I couldn't say his name, even though I wanted to scream it out.

Robinson, come back! I'm not ready! I'm completely, totally not ready!

Leafy's barks took on a tone of wild confusion. I grabbed her by the collar and buried my face in her warm neck, and I thought, *Oh my God, how am I going to tell Lou? How am I going to do anything ever again?*

I had a mouthful of Leafy's hair and she was still barking, but more softly now, dissolving into a pitiful whimper.

It was done. It was over.

And I'd been asleep.

52

A HAND CAME DOWN AND TOUCHED MY shoulder, and I jumped like I'd been burned. I looked up through tear-blurred eyes.

Robinson's face, seeming to float above the bed like a ghost's. And then his familiar low voice. He said, "Axi? Are you okay?"

I nearly fell over. It was him. He was alive. "Do I look okay?" I yelled. I crawled back up onto the bed and gripped his hands as if he'd rescued me from drowning. Never in my life had I been more relieved. "Tell me: *do I look okay?*"

"Your eyes are sort of red," he said, his voice groggy but teasing. "Are you allergic to Leafy or something?"

"I'm going to kill you," I gasped. I let go of his hands and lay down next to him in the bed, pressing myself against his side and trying to calm my breathing. I'd been so close to losing him.

"Oh, you probably won't have to bother," Robinson said. "Something's already on that job. But don't worry. I'm still around to torture you."

"Never stop," I said.

"I'll do my best." Robinson patted the edge of bed, and Leafy hopped up, too, though it was obviously not easy for her. I watched him pet her soft head and ears. He yawned and then moved around in the bed, restless and uncomfortable as he woke up to his sickness and the pain it caused him.

I ran my finger along the side of his cheek. "Do you want anything?" I asked.

He didn't answer me. His eyes closed, and I thought he was falling back to sleep. He'd been sleeping so much lately. As his breathing became more regular, I slowly eased out of the bed and went to the door, ready to check on his parents. Then he said softly, "Yes."

"What?"

"I want more time," he said. His lashes were dark against his pale skin.

I bit my lip and felt the sting of tears again. "Okay," I whispered. "Coming right up."

When I was in the hallway, he called me back.

"Axi," he said, half-sitting up again. "Listen, okay? First thing: Leafy does not need another treat, no matter how much she thinks she does. So leave the Milk-Bones in the pantry.

Second thing: there's a hole in your shirt, and you should get my mom to sew it. Third thing: like that dumb Mason Jennings song says, there are so many ways to die."

I held up a hand. "Whoa, Robinson—"

He ignored me. "It doesn't matter what the end looks like—what matters is that it came. Bam, you're done. But life, Axi? There are degrees of life. You can live it well or half-asleep. You can go sledding down a sand dune, or you can spend your life in front of the TV. And I don't mean to sound like a stupid after-school special, but you have to keep living the way we did these last weeks. Risk, Axi. That's the secret. Risk everything."

I nodded, trying not to cry again. "Okay. But I might not keep stealing cars."

"That's all right," he said.

"What am I going to do—?" I asked. I couldn't say the final two words of the sentence: *without you*.

Robinson smiled. "You should probably try to not fail physics. And you should keep writing."

I thought of my journal, the sloppy, haphazard notes in it and all the pages to be filled. At least I'd taken some pictures on our trip. "I'll write the good parts."

"No, you have to write the good and the bad." Robinson picked at the edge of the blanket. His eyes were so huge and serious. "You can write all about me, and I'll live forever that way."

What could I say? I sank down onto a chair and put my head in my hands.

"You know, yours was the only book I ever wanted to read. So just write it, Axi. You can do it. You can do anything. I mean, look at you. You're not GG anymore—you're so much bigger than her."

I laughed bitterly. "I don't miss her."

"I loved her," Robinson said. "And I loved the sick girl you were when I met you, and I loved the good student and the bad driver. I loved the car thief, the hitchhiker, the quoter of novels I haven't read, and the hater of Slim Jims...Axi Moore, I've loved every you there ever was."

I walked over to the bed and laid my head on his chest. "I'll always be your girl," I whispered.

"I know," he said.

I watched the way our fingers intertwined, and I thought, *What are hands made for but this? For holding. For holding* on.

53

THE DAYS BLURRED INTO ONE ANOTHER as Robinson began to dream more and speak less. Time had lost meaning for him, but I was overcome by a sense of waiting. Something was coming, something that would be dreadful darkness and that would also be relief.

We stayed with him in shifts: Lou in the mornings, Joe in the afternoons, Jonathan in the evenings, and me at night. I read to him from Lou's books: Steinbeck, Whitman, Fitzgerald, Hemingway. She read him *The Little Prince*.

One night, in the middle of my watch, I slipped outside into the warm darkness. The crickets were going crazy, and the lightning bugs were like tiny lanterns flashing a kind of insect Morse code.

Through the window, Robinson looked small and frail under the covers, like a little kid in his childhood bed. Like he ought to be clutching a teddy bear.

I picked a star and wished as hard as I could that somehow I could protect him from what was on the horizon.

We're in this together, Robinson used to say. I remembered the first time he'd ever said it to me, at dinnertime in the cancer ward when we'd been handed a tray of brown slop and green peas. "We're in this together," Robinson had declared. "Axi, we can do this." He'd lifted his fork high in the air, like a sword. "We can eat this...this...whatever it is!"

It was a joke back then; now it was real. We were in this together for just a little bit longer, because what was coming next, Robinson was going to have to go through alone. I would have traded my life for his, but there was no one to offer this to. No one who could make the exchange. No star that would grant my wish.

At three o'clock that morning, I was dozing, my hand on his, when suddenly he was awake.

"The motorcycle," he said, his voice haunted and urgent. "Does it have gas?"

I was instantly at attention. "Yes," I said.

"I think the head gasket's blown—it's seeping oil."

"Your brother's looking into it," I said. Whatever world Robinson was in now, I would play along. "He says not to worry, he'll take care of it. It's going to be up and running right away."

"What about the clutch cable? It's worn."

"He'll fix that, too."

Then Robinson looked at me for a long time. At some point, he seemed to come back to himself. "Axi," he whispered.

"Hi," I whispered back.

He gazed around the room at the Bob Dylan poster, the leaning guitars, all the things he'd left behind when he went away to the hospital. His fingers fluttered, and I reached out to grab them.

I knew what was coming. What I should say.

There was a stone in my throat, but I swallowed hard. "It's okay," I said. "It's okay to go." The final stop.

He brought my hand up to his lips and kissed it, right in the center of my palm. Then he closed my fingers around it, as if the kiss were something I could hold on to forever.

I climbed into bed with him. He shifted, sighing. "Axi," he said.

"I'm right here."

I held his head in my arms. I pressed my mouth to his cheek. *We are in this together.*

"Axi," he said again.

I told him I loved him. He loved me, too, he said—always. And I heard him say my name again. He whispered it over and over until it didn't sound like my name at all anymore. It was only sound, only rhythm. Almost like a song.

"Axi." He sighed. "Axi."

And then, finally, he was silent.

Outside, the song of the crickets seemed to crescendo. I reached into my pocket for the lucky penny I had flipped so long ago in the cancer ward, hoping that it somehow meant Robinson would make it. I'd kept that penny with me every single day after it showed me heads, that he would always be with me.

Now I held it tight, and then I flipped it high into the air and watched it land. But on what, it didn't matter. There was no question anymore, no wish—only the answer, and the emptiness it brings.

epilogue

54

IN BUCOLIC KLAMATH FALLS, EARLY FALL
is bright and dry. The leaves are already turning brown, letting
themselves be blown from their branches into sad little piles on
unmown lawns.

My dad is down in the courtyard, searching for the watch
he dropped on his way home from the bar last night. He's been
looking for half an hour already. (If you ask me, I think Critter
found it and took it straight to Jack's Pawn.) Dad keeps looking
up at me, sitting here on the apartment's tiny balcony, like he
thinks that any minute I might vanish into thin air.

I'm not going anywhere. My first community service session isn't until tomorrow afternoon. See, when I got back
home, the first thing I did was walk to the police station and
turn myself in.

Yup. Once a GG, always a GG.

I think I knew from the moment we stole the Harley that I was going to have to make amends for our journey. It was the right thing to do. And even though Robinson's eyes are likely rolling out of his head right now, I think he might have been smiling down on me, too, when the judge handed me my sentence. Grand theft auto is a felony and usually lands people in jail, but miraculously I was only charged with a misdemeanor and was banned from getting a driver's license until I turn twenty-one, and I'm basically going to do community service until my arms fall off.

It's completely worth it to me. After all, the people who "lent" us their cars gave Robinson and me an incredible gift, and I'll gladly pick up trash for the rest of my life if I have to. In fact, I'm thinking about volunteering for the police department, too.

"Axi," my dad calls up, "shouldn't you be heading to school soon?"

"I'll be down in a minute," I reply. *Ugh.* I'd forgotten about my mandatory physics tutoring session, which starts in an hour. Turns out you can't pass a class when you ditch the last three weeks of it and stop being able to understand the supposedly important laws of physics.

Those laws don't explain why Robinson had to die. They don't explain how I'll keep going without him. So I'm pretty sure I don't care that much about understanding how "the entropy of any isolated system not in thermal equilibrium almost always increases."

But then, like a contrarian voice from the heavens, something from class pops right into my mind: *a body in motion tends to stay in motion; a body at rest tends to stay at rest*. That's the definition of *inertia*, a word that would have made Robinson roll his eyes.

I am in motion. I will stay in motion. Maybe one of those magical forces of the physical universe will kick in and keep me going, no matter how much pain I feel.

Or not.

I wrap my arms around myself, inhaling the scent of Robinson that lingers on his flannel shirt, which I'm wearing. And my tears well up and start to spill out all over again. I'm just really, really tired.

"Hey, Axi, check this out!" my dad calls. I lean over the balcony and he points to a part of the withering rosebush in the yard—one solitary flower still miraculously in bloom. I smile weakly. I was hoping he'd finally found his watch.

"You okay?" he asks.

I shrug. I mean, how am I supposed to answer that question? I saw Dr. Suzuki last week, and my cancer is still in remission. My five-year survival rate? Almost 93 percent.

So technically, yes, I'm okay. *Technically.*

But as I sit here letting the sun warm my face, I know that there's a part of me that's missing. It's as if the doctors had sliced something essential out. A vital part that I was sure I needed to keep me breathing. Not just existing. Even now, sometimes I think I hear Robinson's laughter, and for a moment my heart lifts. But when I turn my head to look, it's never him. It's the wind, or the call of a bird, or a hallucination of my own mad dream.

I think it was love at first sight for both of us; it just took us a little while to figure it out. That was understandable, considering we were being stuck with needles, shot through with radioactive particles, possibly poisoned by the horrific substances the hospital tried to pass off as food, and then, when we got discharged, running away and stealing cars together.

So we had other things on our minds.

Of course, sometimes I think maybe we *did* know our feelings right away, but we couldn't admit them to ourselves. Like we secretly thought, *Okay, cancer is scary, but love is* terrifying.

And it is. But it's also exhilarating and bewildering and miraculous.

Right before Robinson and I left on our trip, I'd written a paper on the French essayist Michel de Montaigne. ("Ooooh, *faaaahncy*," Robinson had teased.) "The greatest thing in the world is to know how to belong to oneself," Montaigne wrote.

And while Montaigne was a very smart man, I'm sure, in this particular instance he's full of shit.

The greatest thing in the world is to know how to belong to someone else. The way Robinson and I belonged to each other. We held on as tight as we could, as long as we could. It wasn't enough.

And yet it has to be.

At night when the stars come out, I look up and remember Robinson at the window of the hospital in La Junta, me standing so close to him that it took my breath away. I think about what I didn't say then, which is this: the stars we see aren't even real stars. We see the light that they gave off millions of years ago but that is only now reaching our eyes. We don't see a star as much as a memory.

"Remember the me before this," a pale, sick Robinson said to me. "Remember the me with the guitar."

And since memory is all I have now—unless you count a glass orb, a key chain, a shirt, and a penny that once was lucky—I tried to do what he asked.

"Write about us," Robinson urged. "Tell our story."

And I did it; I told our story. You hold it in your hands.

I just wish I could have done it better. How can you, through my plain and simple words, possibly experience the joy I felt when Robinson jumped into that Los Angeles pool, sledded on the golden sand of the Great Dunes, or kissed me in an ancient temple? How can you understand what Robinson meant to me? His laugh was like a peal of bells. He really did consider Slim Jims to be their own food group. When he played the guitar and sang, whether it was in the cancer ward or in Tompkins Square Park, everyone stopped to listen. He was magic.

"Axi!" my dad shouts from below. "I found it!" He's holding up his Timex and grinning like it's a winning lottery ticket.

"Good for you!" I call down. As if he's the kid and I'm the mom.

I feel like I owe my dad, running off the way I did. He almost drank himself to death, worrying and missing me. I'm trying to make up for the fact that I barely got back in time to save him.

I only wish I could have saved Robinson, too.

But I know Robinson didn't want me to be broken after his death. He wanted me whole, well, and writing. About us.

"Make sure to throw in a lot of words I wouldn't under-stand," he'd said — using the last bits of his energy to tease me. "And a lot of fancy metaphors and stuff."

I just nodded. I'd do anything he wanted.

Loving Robinson made everything seem brighter and more beautiful. And if life has faded a little since he's been gone, it's still a lot more vivid than it used to be. Now the sun dazzles. That vermilion rose flings its perfume into the air. And the breeze soothes me, if I let it.

Most days I think of him and smile, even if I have to cry my eyes out first. He never stopped believing he was lucky.

Maybe not lucky enough to survive, but lucky simply to have lived.

He was my light, my heart, my beautiful scalawag. And I was—I *am*—his GG.

OSCAR JAMES ROBINSON

JUNE 21, 1996–JULY 6, 2013

Missing me one place, search another.
I stop somewhere waiting for you.

—Walt Whitman

FIND OUT HOW
THE CONFESSIONS
BEGAN...

AND WHAT REALLY
HAPPENED TO
MALCOLM AND
MAUD ANGEL.

TURN THE PAGE FOR A PREVIEW.

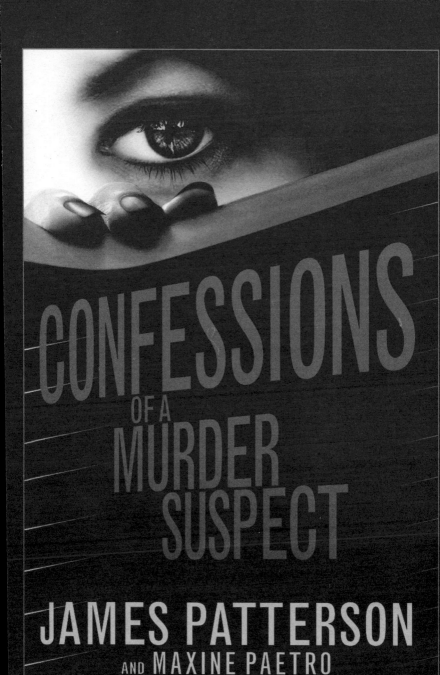

CONFESSIONS
OF A
MURDER
SUSPECT

JAMES PATTERSON
AND MAXINE PAETRO

1

I have some really bad secrets to share with someone, and it might as well be you—a stranger, a reader of books, but most of all, a person who can't hurt me. So here goes nothing, or maybe everything. I'm not sure if I can even tell the difference anymore.

The night my parents died—after they'd been carried out in slick black body bags through the service elevator—my brother Matthew shouted at the top of his powerful lungs, "My parents were vile, but they didn't deserve to be taken out with the *trash*!"

He was right about the last part—and, as things turned out, the first part as well.

But I'm getting ahead of myself, aren't I? Please forgive me....I do that a lot.

I'd been asleep downstairs, directly under my parents' bedroom, when it happened. So I never heard a thing—no frantic thumping, no terrified shouting, no fracas at all. I woke up to the scream of sirens speeding up Central Park West, maybe one of the most common sounds in New York City.

But that night it was different.

The sirens stopped *right downstairs*. That was what caused me to wake up with a hundred-miles-an-hour heartbeat. Was the building on fire? Did some old neighbor have a stroke?

I threw off my double layer of blankets, went to my window, and looked down to the street, nine dizzying floors below. I saw three police cruisers and what could have been an unmarked police car parked on Seventy-second Street, right at the front gates of our apartment building, the exclusive and infamous Dakota.

A moment later our intercom buzzed, a jarring *blat-blat* that punched right through my flesh and bones.

Why was the doorman paging *us*? This was *crazy*.

My bedroom was the one closest to the front door, so I bolted through the living room, hooked a right at the sharks in the aquarium coffee table, and passed between Robert and his nonstop TV.

When I reached the foyer, I stabbed at the intercom button to stop the irritating blare before it woke up the whole house.

I spoke in a loud whisper to the doorman through the speaker: "Sal? What's happening?"

"Miss Tandy? Two policemen are on the way up to your apartment right now. I couldn't stop them. They got a nine-one-one call. It's an emergency. That's what they said."

"There's been a mistake, Sal. Everyone is asleep here. It's after midnight. How could you let them up?"

Before Sal could answer, the doorbell rang, and then fists pounded the door. A harsh masculine voice called out, "This is the police."

I made sure the chain was in place and then opened the door—but just a crack.

I peered out through the opening and saw two men in the hallway. The older one was as big as a bear but kind of soft-looking and spongy. The younger one was wiry and had a sharp, expressionless face, something like a hatchet blade, or . . . no, a hatchet blade is exactly right.

The younger one flashed his badge and said, "Sergeant

Capricorn Caputo and Detective Ryan Hayes, NYPD. Please open the door."

Capricorn Caputo? I thought. *Seriously?* "You've got the wrong apartment," I said. "No one here called the police."

"Open the door, miss. And I mean *right now.*"

"I'll get my parents," I said through the crack. I had no idea that my parents were dead and that we would be the only serious suspects in a double homicide. I was in my last moment of innocence.

But who am I kidding? No one in the Angel family was ever innocent.

2

"*Open up,* or my partner will kick down the door!" Hatchet Face called out.

It is no exaggeration to say that my whole family was about to get a wake-up call from *hell*. But all I was thinking at that particular moment was that the police could *not* kick down the door. This was the *Dakota*. We could get *evicted* for allowing someone to disturb the peace.

I unlatched the chain and swung the door open. I was wearing pajamas, of course; chick-yellow ones with dinosaurs chasing butterflies. Not exactly what I would have chosen for a meeting with the police.

Detective Hayes, the bearish one, said, "What's your name?"

"Tandy Angel."

"Are you the daughter of Malcolm and Maud Angel?"

"I am. Can you please tell me why you're here?"

"Tandy is your real name?" he said, ignoring my question.

"I'm called Tandy. Please wait here. I'll get my parents to talk to you."

"We'll go with you," said Sergeant Caputo.

Caputo's grim expression told me that this was not a request. I turned on lights as we headed toward my parents' bedroom suite.

I was climbing the circular stairwell, thinking that my parents were going to kill me for bringing these men upstairs, when suddenly both cops pushed rudely past me. By the time I had reached my parents' room, the overhead light was on and the cops were bending over my parents' bed.

Even with Caputo and Hayes in the way, I could see that my mother and father looked all wrong. Their sheets and blankets were on the floor, and their nightclothes were bunched under their arms, as if they'd tried to take them off. My father's arm looked like it had been twisted out of its socket. My mother was lying facedown across my father's body, and her tongue was sticking out of her mouth. It had turned *black*.

I didn't need a coroner to tell me that they were dead. I knew it just moments after I saw them. Diagnosis certain.

I shrieked and ran toward them, but Hayes stopped me cold. He kept me out of the room, putting his big paws on my shoulders and forcibly walking me backward out to the hallway.

"I'm sorry to do this," he said, then shut the bedroom door in my face.

I didn't try to open it. I just stood there. Motionless. Almost not breathing.

So, you might be wondering why I wasn't bawling, screeching, or passing out from shock and horror. Or why I wasn't running to the bathroom to vomit or curling up in the fetal position, hugging my knees and sobbing. Or doing any of the things that a teenage girl who's just seen her murdered parents' bodies ought to do.

The answer is complicated, but here's the simplest way to say it: I'm not a whole lot like most girls. At least, not from what I can tell. For me, having a meltdown was seriously out of the question.

From the time I was two, when I first started speaking in paragraphs that began with topic sentences, Malcolm and Maud had told me that I was exceptionally smart. Later, they told me that I was analytical and focused, and that my detachment from watery emotion was a superb trait. They said that if I nurtured these qualities, I would achieve or even exceed my extraordinary potential, and this wasn't just a good thing, but a great thing. It was the only thing that mattered, in fact.

It was a challenge, and I had accepted it.

That's why I was more prepared for this catastrophe than most kids my age would be, or maybe *any* kids my age.

Yes, it was true that panic was shooting up and down my spine and zinging out to my fingertips. I was shocked, maybe even terrified. But I quickly tamped down the screaming voice inside my head and collected my wits, along with the few available facts.

One: My parents had died in some unspeakable way.

Two: Someone had known about their deaths and called the police.

Three: Our doors were locked, and there had been no obvious break-in. Aside from me, my brothers Harry and Hugo and my mother's personal assistant, Samantha, were the only ones home.

I went downstairs and got my phone. I called both my uncle Peter and our lawyer, Philippe Montaigne. Then I went to each of my siblings' bedrooms, and to Samantha's, too. And somehow, I told them each the inexpressibly horrible news that our mother and father were dead, and that it was possible they'd been murdered.

3

Can you imagine the words you'd use, dear reader, to tell your family that your parents had been murdered? I hope so, because I'm not going to be able to share those wretched moments with you right now. We're just getting to know each other, and I take a little bit of time to warm up to people. Can you be patient with me? I promise it'll be worth the wait.

After I'd completed that horrible task—perhaps the worst task of my life—I tried to focus my fractured attention back on Sergeant Capricorn Caputo. He was a rough-looking character, like a bad cop in a black-and-white film from the forties who smoked unfiltered cigarettes, had stained fingers, and was coughing up his lungs on his way to the cemetery.

Caputo looked to be about thirty-five years old. He had one continuous eyebrow, a furry ledge over his stony black eyes. His thin lips were set in a short, hard line. He had rolled up the sleeves of his shiny blue jacket, and I noted a zodiac sign tattooed on his wrist.

He looked like *exactly* the kind of detective I wanted to have working on the case of my murdered parents.

Gnarly and mean.

Detective Hayes was an entirely different cat. He had a basically pleasant, faintly lined face and wore a wedding ring, an NYPD Windbreaker, and steel-tipped boots. He looked sympathetic to us kids, sitting in a stunned semicircle around him. But Detective Hayes wasn't in charge, and he wasn't doing the talking.

Caputo stood with his back to our massive fireplace and coughed into his fist. Then he looked around the living room with his mouth wide open.

He couldn't believe how we lived.

And I can't say I blame him.

He took in the eight-hundred-gallon aquarium coffee table with the four glowing pygmy sharks swimming circles around their bubbler.

His jaw dropped even farther when he saw the life-size merman hanging by its tail from a bloody hook and chain in the ceiling near the staircase.

He sent a glance across the white-lacquered grand piano, which we called "Pegasus" because it looked like it had wings.

And he stared at Robert, who was slumped over in a La-Z-Boy with a can of Bud in one hand and a remote control in the other, just watching the static on his TV screen.

Robert is a remarkable creation. He really is. It's next to impossible to tell that he, his La-Z-Boy, and his very own TV are all part of an incredibly lifelike, technologically advanced sculpture. He was cast from a real person, then rendered in polyvinyl and an auto-body filler composite called Bondo. Robert looks so real, you half expect him to crunch his beer can against his forehead and ask for another cold one.

"What's the point of this thing?" Detective Caputo asked.

"It's an artistic style called hyperrealism," I responded.

"Hyper-real, huh?" Detective Caputo said. "Does that mean 'over-the-top'? Because that's kind of a theme in this family, isn't it?"

No one answered him. To us, this was home.

When Detective Caputo was through taking in the décor, he fixed his eyes on each of us in turn. We just blinked at him. There were no hysterics. In fact, there was no apparent emotion at all.

"Your parents were *murdered*," he said. "Do you get that? What's the matter? No one here loved them?"

We did love them, but it wasn't a simple love. To start with, my parents were complicated: strict, generous, punishing, expansive, withholding. And as a result, we were complicated, too. I knew all of us felt what I was feeling—an internal tsunami of horror and loss and confusion. But we couldn't show it. Not even to save our lives.

Of course, Sergeant Caputo didn't see us as bereaved children going through the worst day of our tender young lives. He saw us as *suspects*, every one of us a "person of interest" in a locked-door double homicide.

He didn't try to hide his judgment, and I couldn't fault his reasoning.

I thought he was right.

My parents' killer was in that room.

JAMES PATTERSON
BOOK**SHOTS**

stories at the speed of life

BOOK**SHOTS** are page-turning stories by James Patterson and other writers that can be read in one sitting.

Each and every one is fast-paced, 100% story-driven; a shot of pure entertainment guaranteed to satisfy.

Under 150 pages
Under £3

Available as new, compact paperbacks, ebooks and audio, everywhere books are sold.

For more details, visit: **www.bookshots.com**

BOOK**SHOTS**
**THE ULTIMATE FORM OF STORYTELLING.
FROM THE ULTIMATE STORYTELLER.**

Also by James Patterson

ALEX CROSS NOVELS

Along Came a Spider • Kiss the Girls • Jack and Jill • Cat and Mouse •
Pop Goes the Weasel • Roses are Red • Violets are Blue • Four Blind Mice •
The Big Bad Wolf • London Bridges • Mary, Mary • Cross • Double Cross •
Cross Country • Alex Cross's Trial (*with Richard DiLallo*) • I, Alex Cross •
Cross Fire • Kill Alex Cross • Merry Christmas, Alex Cross • Alex Cross,
Run • Cross My Heart • Hope to Die • Cross Justice • Cross the Line

THE WOMEN'S MURDER CLUB SERIES

1st to Die • 2nd Chance (*with Andrew Gross*) • 3rd Degree (*with Andrew
Gross*) • 4th of July (*with Maxine Paetro*) • The 5th Horseman (*with Maxine
Paetro*) • The 6th Target (*with Maxine Paetro*) • 7th Heaven (*with Maxine
Paetro*) • 8th Confession (*with Maxine Paetro*) • 9th Judgement (*with Maxine
Paetro*) • 10th Anniversary (*with Maxine Paetro*) • 11th Hour (*with Maxine
Paetro*) • 12th of Never (*with Maxine Paetro*) • Unlucky 13 (*with Maxine Paetro*)
• 14th Deadly Sin (*with Maxine Paetro*) • 15th Affair (*with Maxine Paetro*)

DETECTIVE MICHAEL BENNETT SERIES

Step on a Crack (*with Michael Ledwidge*) • Run for Your Life (*with Michael
Ledwidge*) • Worst Case (*with Michael Ledwidge*) • Tick Tock (*with Michael
Ledwidge*) • I, Michael Bennett (*with Michael Ledwidge*) • Gone (*with
Michael Ledwidge*) • Burn (*with Michael Ledwidge*) • Alert (*with
Michael Ledwidge*) • Bullseye (*with Michael Ledwidge*)

PRIVATE NOVELS

Private (*with Maxine Paetro*) • Private London (*with Mark Pearson*) •
Private Games (*with Mark Sullivan*) • Private: No. 1 Suspect (*with Maxine
Paetro*) • Private Berlin (*with Mark Sullivan*) • Private Down Under (*with
Michael White*) • Private L.A. (*with Mark Sullivan*) • Private India (*with
Ashwin Sanghi*) • Private Vegas (*with Maxine Paetro*) • Private Sydney (*with
Kathryn Fox*) • Private Paris (*with Mark Sullivan*) • The Games (*with Mark
Sullivan*) • Private Delhi (*with Ashwin Sanghi*)

NYPD RED SERIES

NYPD Red (*with Marshall Karp*) • NYPD Red 2 (*with Marshall Karp*) •
NYPD Red 3 (*with Marshall Karp*) • NYPD Red 4 (*with Marshall Karp*)

STAND-ALONE THRILLERS

Sail (*with Howard Roughan*) • Swimsuit (*with Maxine Paetro*) •
Don't Blink (*with Howard Roughan*) • Postcard Killers (*with Liza
Marklund*) • Toys (*with Neil McMahon*) • Now You See Her (*with Michael
Ledwidge*) • Kill Me If You Can (*with Marshall Karp*) • Guilty Wives (*with
David Ellis*) • Zoo (*with Michael Ledwidge*) • Second Honeymoon (*with
Howard Roughan*) • Mistress (*with David Ellis*) • Invisible (*with David
Ellis*) • The Thomas Berryman Number • Truth or Die (*with
Howard Roughan*) • Murder House (*with David Ellis*) • Never Never (*with
Candice Fox*) • Woman of God (*with Maxine Paetro*)

NON-FICTION

Torn Apart (*with Hal and Cory Friedman*) •
The Murder of King Tut (*with Martin Dugard*)

ROMANCE

Sundays at Tiffany's (*with Gabrielle Charbonnet*) •
The Christmas Wedding (*with Richard DiLallo*)

OTHER TITLES

Miracle at Augusta (*with Peter de Jonge*)

FAMILY OF PAGE-TURNERS

MIDDLE SCHOOL BOOKS

The Worst Years of My Life (*with Chris Tebbetts*) • Get Me Out of Here! (*with
Chris Tebbetts*) • My Brother Is a Big, Fat Liar (*with Lisa Papademetriou*) • How
I Survived Bullies, Broccoli, and Snake Hill (*with Chris Tebbetts*) • Ultimate
Showdown (*with Julia Bergen*) • Save Rafe! (*with Chris Tebbetts*) • Just My
Rotten Luck (*with Chris Tebbetts*) • Dog's Best Friend (*with Chris Tebbetts*)

I FUNNY SERIES

I Funny (*with Chris Grabenstein*) •
I Even Funnier (*with Chris Grabenstein*) •
I Totally Funniest (*with Chris Grabenstein*) •
I Funny TV (*with Chris Grabenstein*)

TREASURE HUNTERS SERIES

Treasure Hunters (*with Chris Grabenstein*) •
Danger Down the Nile (*with Chris Grabenstein*) •
Secret of the Forbidden City (*with Chris Grabenstein*) •
Peril at the Top of the World (*with Chris Grabenstein*)

HOUSE OF ROBOTS SERIES

House of Robots (*with Chris Grabenstein*) •
Robots Go Wild! (*with Chris Grabenstein*) •
Robot Revolution (*with Chris Grabenstein*)

OTHER ILLUSTRATED NOVELS

Kenny Wright: Superhero (*with Chris Tebbetts*) •
Homeroom Diaries (*with Lisa Papademetriou*) • Jacky Ha-Ha
(*with Chris Grabenstein*) • Word of Mouse (*with Chris Grabenstein*)

DANIEL X SERIES

The Dangerous Days of Daniel X (*with Michael Ledwidge*) • Watch the
Skies (*with Ned Rust*) • Demons and Druids (*with Adam Sadler*) •
Game Over (*with Ned Rust*) • Armageddon (*with Chris Grabenstein*) •
Lights Out (*with Chris Grabenstein*)

GRAPHIC NOVELS

Daniel X: Alien Hunter (*with Leopoldo Gout*) •
Maximum Ride: Manga Vols. 1–9 (*with NaRae Lee*)

For more information about James Patterson's novels, visit
www.jamespatterson.co.uk

Or become a fan on Facebook